GET A JOB

MIKE ROBERTSON

authorHOUSE®

AuthorHouse™
1663 Liberty Drive
Bloomington, IN 47403
www.authorhouse.com
Phone: 833-262-8899

Published by AuthorHouse 03/24/2022

ISBN: 978-1-6655-5583-8 (sc)
ISBN: 978-1-6655-5584-5 (e)

Library of Congress Control Number: 2022905590

CONTENTS

A WARNING TO COME

He was a born clerk, a menial worker, adept at little more than unskilled labour. Either one of those things or he was just plain unlucky, or just plain dumb. It only took him several years of taking advantage of a generous unemployment insurance program before he was to arrive at any one of those conclusions. Before that, it was relatively low grades in school, mediocre opinions from teachers, a below average disciplinary record, and parents who didn't have any money to influence their son's academic record. Besides, they didn't have a high opinion of him anyway. On the other hand, he was facing a fate that he was convinced that many with a similar background or a similar lack of ambition would eventually suffer. He basically took up his career as a clerk after he realized that he likely had no other choice. The background was a banality that reflected bad history, an addiction to the ease of his own past an adequate explanation. He faced it. He may have had no other choice or so he thought. Maybe the previous generation had been right although their unfortunate circumstances were certainly less hospitable to the laziness that he was now pursuing. They had the depression and a world war. For his part, he had the suburbs, terrible television shows and parents who didn't force him to go to work when he was thirteen years old. It was fortunate that he could pursue constant indolence without interruption, at least until he was on his own and had no other choice. Unlike some of his university colleagues, he had few career aspirations, if any. In addition, he had few job qualifications, unless prospective employers regarded the composition of poetry and a sense of humor adequate qualifications to hire someone.

He was maybe five years removed from leaving university, four years removed from marrying a woman named Sharon, and less than a year removed from being asked by Sharon to leave her presence for good. It was a situation that could easily have overwhelmed him into a state close to destitution. Sure, he had managed to occupy a number of relatively inconsequential though responsible positions without any difficulty over the past several years, including at least two of which may have had a future. Still, he usually lost interest in each of those jobs, prompting him to turn to unemployment insurance payments while he was supposedly looking for gainful employment.

In this particular instance, several months unemployed after being laid off by Mr. Brennan of the Ottawa Car Rental, he really didn't have a choice. He had a couple of months to secure gainful employment, no matter how depressing that prognosis, or face a charge of criminal fraud, a dreadful prospect that scared the hell out of him.

The threatened charge was making phony claims to the Unemployment Insurance Commission (UIC), a government agency that made not having a job less embarrassing than it may have been in the past. Specifically, the false assertions he allegedly made involved informing the agency, in writing mind you, that he had applied for positions when in fact he had not, the problem being that the statements were easily verified as prevarications. Apparently, in order to receive unemployment benefits, one had to provide evidence of actively looking for work, a requirement that he had ignored. So when he was advised by an official during an interview at the UIC office on Carling Avenue in Ottawa that not only were his benefits immediately terminated, leaving him significantly short of cash, but he could face criminal charges, he panicked. His reaction was understandable, if not predictable. At first, he foolishly contemplated suicide but eventually settled on getting drunk with a friend who fortunately had recently graduated from UIC to welfare. It was sometime in June of the year 1975 or 1976. For some reason, he had tried to forget the precise year.

THE EARLY YEARS
THE WORK ETHIC TRAINING I

His first job, if one could call it a job, was caddying at the Beaconsfield Golf Club. He applied for the position at his mother's suggestion. Apparently, one of her patients, she was an emergency room nurse at a local hospital, originally made the suggestion and she had relayed it to her son, it being more than a suggestion, his mother being a woman of considerable conviction. The first day, the day he applied for the job, he rode his bicycle over to the golf course, which was on Cartier Avenue in Pointe Claire. His mother forced him to wear a stupid green straw hat on which she had painted a number of golf related words and expressions, such as birdie, fore, putt, and playing through, all suggested he assumed by his father who used to play the game regularly. Mike Butler was embarrassed with the hat but continued to wear it because he was worried that his mother would somehow find out that he wasn't. That first day, when he climbed the backstairs of the caddy stack, past maybe a dozen boys waiting to catch a bag, he was almost faint with shame. Four or five of them, including two older guys who were seated on wooden boxes at the top of the stairs playing cards, sneered at him. One called him a "bag rat" while three simply pointed out his hat to the rest of them. They all laughed.

There was an older guy behind a Dutch door beyond which was a small office with golf pennants and calendars on the walls, a desk and a chair, several small plastic trophies and a filing cabinet. Mike noticed that a sign identifying the occupant as the "Caddy Master" was attached to the top half of the Dutch door. The man behind the desk in the office was smoking, chewing gum and swigging from a small coke bottle. Predictably, he was wearing a blue golf shirt on which a red insignia "Beaconsfield Golf Club" was written under his left breast pocket. The golf shirt looked like it had not been laundered in weeks, though it was decorated by mustard and grass stains. He was also sporting a tattoo, an unusual skin design for anyone in 1964, unless one was in either the navy or prison. Having slipped past the older guys playing cards, Mike was leaning on the bottom half of the Dutch door when the "Caddy Master" first noticed him. He got up and came from around the desk to greet him.

"Help you." he barked at him. Mike was a trifle intimidated, up close the "Caddy Master" looked like he had the tattoo applied in prison rather in the navy. "Are you in charge of the caddies?" Mike asked in an understandably timid voice. The "Caddy Master" didn't seem to hear him. Mike raised his voice somewhat and asked again. "Right. I'm Ken and I run the caddies." said the "Caddy Master". "Are you looking to pick up some caddy work? " Mike replied, "Hope so." Ken asked, "Okay. You know golf?", the question in lieu of an application Mike guessed. It seemed the sole qualification for the job, aside of course from an ability to carry golf clubs. He had assumed, or had been told by his father who was at least a golfer, that a caddy had to know something about golf as to be in a position to offer advice, if asked, which seemed a little ridiculous when he thought about it. So he was qualified. He had played golf, maybe a couple of dozen rounds total, and had occasionally watched golf on television with the old man.

"Sure, I have played a few times and watch it on television." proclaimed Mike. Ken started to laugh. "Good, I'm glad but I don't care. If you can carry a golf bag, I'll put you on the roster." The "Caddy Master" paused for a moment and then asked him his name. He gave it and Ken wrote it down." By the way, Mike, every round you get, you'll have to give Roger a tip. And oh yeah, get rid of that dumb hat." "Who's Roger?" asked Mike. Ken pointed to one of the two old guys playing cards at the top of stairs.

———

For the remainder of that summer, Mike Butler carried golf bags for various members of the Beaconsfield Golf Club and their guests. He received $1.50 a round, a free soda at the snack bar between the eleventh and twelfth holes, plus a gratuity, usually fifty cents to a dollar, less the quarter he gave Roger after every round for which he carried clubs. He also would earn the occasional extra $1.00 from the club professional, a middle aged blowhard named Cantwell who would ask some of the younger caddies, including Mike, to stand on the unoccupied fairway of the first hole and shag balls that he would hit from the first tee. They would collect the balls in a small canvas bucket, return them to Cantwell, who then hit them back at the caddies. Cantwell would cackle like an idiot anytime he came close to hitting one of them. As for Mike, he got a three iron in the shin, for which Cantwell gave him an extra quarter, telling him to treat his girlfriend to popcorn at the movies. Another peculiar experience through which he was to suffer was to caddy for club members who had decided that a round of golf was an ideal opportunity to get inebriated, a situation that usually ended with Mike having to ensure that the intoxicated member finished his round without serious mishap, one particularly interesting misadventure being the occasion during which a member named Gallagher almost drowned in a water hazard on a fourteenth hole.

His caddying days ended, however, when one of the golfers refused to pay him because he "didn't like the cut of his jib", a reference about which Mike did not have a clue. He complained to "Caddy Master" Ken who yelled at him for a couple of minutes and then told him not to bring it up again. When Mike informed his mother Ethel, she contacted the president of the club, a former mayor of the municipality in which the golf course was situated, to give him "a piece of her mind". Despite his mother's efforts, Mike was not rehired. Unfortunately, Mike eventually calculated that first job earned him maybe fifty cents an hour for the eight weeks he managed to work that summer. In total, he calculated that he had made around $300 that summer, not bad he thought for a fifteen year old whose previous earnings amounted to fifty cents a week allowance from his parents. It had been a pleasant summer. He had managed to attract a girlfriend, a blonde named Susan.

His first real job, that is the first position for which he was given specific hours, specific duties, reported to a boss, and was paid an hourly wage for services rendered, was working Saturdays as a salesman in the men's wear section of a downtown Montreal department store. He got the job through his father, who was working in the same department store although not in men's wear. His father also told him that that summer would be the last one during which he would be free of full time employment. Next summer, he would have to obtain a full time summer job, that is if he intended to attend college the next year. Otherwise, he would have to get a full time job, pay rent or get a full time job and live on his own. But for now, working one Saturday a week would be enough. He started on the first Saturday in April in the year 1966. He was to graduate from high school in three months.

On his first day on the job, he reported to the personnel office of the T. Eaton Company, the department store situated on St. Catherine Street in downtown Montreal. He went to the main personnel office and was ushered in to talk to a woman named Frances Tremblay who told him to sign a form, handed him his own punch card, told him to go to the fifth floor to use it, and told him to report to the men's wear department on the second floor. When he emerged from one of the dozen elevators on the fifth floor, he found himself standing in front of a battery of punch clocks behind which were literally hundreds of individual punch cards. Mike Butler punched in at 8:15 in the morning. On the second floor, he reported to a man named Jean Carriere, the assistant manager of the men's wear department. He was a relatively thin man wearing a fashionable gray suit over a white shirt with a violet pattern tie and a matching pocket square. He had a full head of black hair and was sporting a pencil mustache which made him look older than he may have been. He looked like he belonged in a movie from the 1940's. He shook Mike's hand and introduced him to the five other staff members in the men's wear, specifically four salesmen and a cashier named Lorraine. They all greeted him with smiles, although all but Lorraine came forward to shake his hand, Lorraine standing with her cigarette behind a cash register on a raised platform. Fact was that three of the five were smoking cigarettes. It reminded Mike of the kind of arrangement that one usually saw in a pharmacy, with the pharmacist standing above the customers behind some sort of barrier. It was like customers were begging the cashier to pay for the things they wanted to buy. Weird he thought.

Pleasantries exchanged, Mr. Carriere then escorted Mike to a specific section of the department, an alcove in which all teen fashions for boys were displayed, the blue jeans, the corduroys, the striped bell bottoms trousers, the velour shirts and sweaters, with paisley designs on practically everything. As Mr. Carriere explained, the salesmen who worked in the alcove were responsible for playing records, greeting customers and managing all sales of merchandise for sale in the alcove. As Carriere was showing Mike the alcove, a tall good looking black man stopped by and Carriere introduced him. His name was Clark and he was the manager of the entire second floor, including the men's wear department. Carriere mentioned Mike's father, who worked in the notions department on the ground floor. Clark smiled, patted Mike on his shoulder and walked away to attend to his responsibilities on the second floor.

As nervous as he was on that first day, he managed to survive the day without apparent difficulty. Aside from his lack of familiarity with the merchandise, the sizes, and the the prices, a twenty minute tutorial from Carriere was hardly sufficient to qualify himself as an effective salesman. He did, however, manage to make more than a dozen sales that first day, maybe a couple of hundred dollars worth, all but two transactions paid in cash, the other two on Eaton credit cards. Since paying for anything by a credit card, whether Eaton's or Visa or American Express or Diner;s Club, was unusual in 1966, Mike had to seek Lorraine's assistance to complete the transactions. Aside from possible problems with credit cards, a more significant problem he encountered involved, not surprisingly, language. He understood that most of the salesmen were bilingual, French and English speaking, almost a requirement for a major department store in Montreal in 1966. Unfortunately, Mike Butler was hardly linguistically qualified, his French language skills close to pathetic, if not non-existent. It was unlikely that Mike would have been hired at all unless his father had not vouched for him. That first day, four customers spoke to him in French, three of whom switched to English as soon as he apologetically explained that he could not speak French, the other allowed an unpleasant look to appear on his face, turned and started to leave the floor. Mike had tried to convince one of his colleagues, all the others on the floor spoke French, to speak to the dissatisfied customer but she was gone before the colleague could arrive.

His father claimed to be bilingual although he was hardly fluent, speaking a halting, stumbling French that may have been efficient enough to be understood, as long as the conversation was limited to the issues relevant to the store and did not get too complicated. On the other hand, despite years of hardly inspired instruction, both in elementary and high school, Mike wasn't even close to being conversant in French, a measurable deficiency, his report card marks for French were his worst. A couple of years later, in his first year in college, his academic performance in French was so bad that he was placed in a remedial French language course with American and Asian students. This of course exposed him to all sorts of snide remarks from a French professor who was a serious supporter of the nascent provincial political party, the Parti Quebecois. Not that it mattered. He failed the same course twice. As an adult, he later reflected on that particular failing, wishing that he had joined a French language team when he was a kid playing bantam and midget hockey. It might have done his career some good.

For the first four or five Saturdays working in the men's wear department, Mike Butler made some important and well known observations. It was confirmed to him that women did most of the purchasing of men's clothes, either on their own or with their husbands in tow, the latter almost a situation comedy of men standing as silent bystanders, pretending to be actually interested in the proceedings. In most cases, wives, and most of them were wives, could have dressed their husbands and/or partners in evening gowns, and there would be no complaints from them. In fact, Mike sometimes found himself, a seventeen year old whose expertise in men's haberdashery was limited to an Eaton brand suit, the owner of a blue blazer, two dress trousers and several shirts, and a half dozen neckties that were passed down from his father who himself was a fairly snappy dresser, as compared to most of his adult men in the neighbourhood. After all, he did work in a department store.

There were a number of other curious things that occurred during Mike Butler's tenure in the men's wear department. Every Saturday morning, before the store opened, one of the women from retail display would report to the department to review the clothing items that were being worn by the mannequins on the floor. Sometimes, a young decorator, whose name was Suzanne, would discuss her suggestions for changing the clothing on the mannequins with Mike, who was unaware of her reasoning but appreciative of it nevertheless. On the other hand, Carriere would inevitably come by and ensure that her skirt, which was Mary Quant short anyway, was as short as possible by actually pushing it higher. Suzanne would titter nervously and look uncomfortable. Any man in the vicinity would snicker while cashier Lorraine would reproach any man loudly enough to attract the attention of the staff in the adjacent section, men's footwear.

But the most significant event that would befall him during his period of employment was a fairly serious fraud that involved at least two members of the men's wear sales staff, full timers that Mike barely knew, only working with them every second Saturday. It would eventually lead to his termination. This began when, after several weeks on the job, he become aware of certain activities by some staff members that store management would not appreciate. According to gossip, rumours that were often substantiated, if not confirmed, by most of his colleagues, if not his boss Mr. Carriere, that maybe as many as dozens of employees, would punch in on the fifth floor and immediately leave to pursue other activities, possibly other positions in other companies. Even Mike's father confirmed that he knew of a couple of guys who had pulled the punch card stunt.

But Mike never participated in the punch card dodge. He had tried something else. He was in his third month of working Saturdays when a grim looking man walked up to him, pointed to some sort of badge that he was wearing on his belt, and introduced himself as store security. He accused him of stealing from the store, suggesting that he was involved somehow with fellow salesmen in a counterfeit refund scheme. According to the security man, the salesmen, who were permanent employees and with whom Mike had little contact, were writing refunds on merchandise that were never purchased and therefore should never have been returned. Working with an associate or associates masquerading as a customer or customers, the salesmen would write phony refunds and the bogus customers would report to the financial office on the first floor to receive the refund in cash. Apparently, the plan had been active for a couple of months and might have cost the store possibly thousands. The two salesmen who were implicated, evidence of which was not shared by the security officer with Mike, were immediately fired and arrested by the police. Finally, the security officer told Mike that the store had to terminate the other four salesmen who worked in men's wear, including him, because they were not convinced that the scheme was limited to the two salesman about whom they had evidence of writing the fraudulent refunds.

Mike was shocked, scared and strangely enough relieved. He had not expected anything of the sort. While he was aware of the usual rumours of misconduct in the store, the punch clock masquerade for one, and had come to believe that some of the department's employees may be liberating merchandise from the store, he had never conceived of a plan like the refund scheme. It was a plan that could easily have been concocted for a crime show on television, it was that audacious. Notwithstanding his fascination with the plan, which was considerable when he thought about it, he was also distressed by the outcome of the discovery of the scheme, specifically that he was to lose his job, an outcome that was sure to anger his father, not only for being fired from a job that he had managed to acquire for him, regardless of the circumstances, his own culpability, or lack of culpability would be irrelevant. The old man would be irate to say the least. As for his mother, she would be irate if his father was.

But he was also relieved with his termination, since his termination would forestall store security from uncovering his own misbehaviour as far as the store was concerned, an irony on which he would reflect for years afterward. Mike was worried that the grim looking guy with a store badge on his belt would eventually find out that he was also stealing from the store. It was minor, the theft of a couple of bucks every now and then but it was theft nonetheless. The scheme was simple. If customers paid cash for relatively low priced items, anything less than five dollars was his usual standard, he would provide the customers with a phony receipt, abandoned receipts retrieved from cashier Lorraine's wastebasket the source, and pocket the cash. Over the three or so months Mike had worked Saturdays, he figured that he might have pocketed $50.00 or so illicitly, easily more than he had lifted from his mother's purse over the same period. While Mike did not suspect that anybody was aware of his occasional thievery, Brian Graham, one of his classmates, had once told him that he had been entrapped by the manager of a local Woolworth's where he had once worked after using a marked $5.00 bill he had stolen to buy a hamburger and a coke at the store's snack bar. Brian liked to tell the story, regardless of its conclusion. He said that the store manager would not allow him to finish his hamburger before firing him. Everybody laughed at that.

On his way home after his anticipatory termination, on an earlier commuter train than he would normally take had he not been asked to leave the building, he contemplated the story he would tell his parents, particularly his father who would likely have a coronary. Fortunately or unfortunately, he didn't know which, his father was working that Saturday, every second Saturday, his routine for as long as Mike could remember. He wondered whether he had been informed of his son's dismissal. In any event, he would require an explanation. After developing a number of possible justifications for losing his job, he settled on an unfortunate incident with a customer, an outburst of bad behaviour that he intended to blame on being intoxicated that afternoon, a few beers at lunch with a guy who worked in deliveries. Mike had recognized him a month earlier. Although several years older than Mike, he recalled him as one of his classmates in grade six. He was one of the three or four grade school flunkies who continually failed until they reached sixteen and could then leave school without attracting the attention of a truant officer. His name was Rick McPhee. Back then, at Saint John Fisher Elementary, everybody knew him. He smoked, wore a leather jacket, had brilliantined hair, and rode to school on a motorcycle. He attracted a lot of attention, was always in trouble with the teachers and the principal and was the subject of significant rumours and innuendos, all of which both titillated and frightened his classmates.

It was must have been at least five years since he had seen him. Mike recognized him one day when he appeared on the second floor to pick up a recent purchase for delivery. Mike immediately knew who he was, he hadn't changed much, and called out to him. Now almost as tall as Rick, Mike was not intimated as he had been when they were both in grade six but was a trifle ingratiating nonetheless. After all, this was the guy who used to frighten the hell out of everyone, even Principal Sinclair who himself used to terrorize the student body like he was a prison warden. Rick seemed pleased to be recognized. He then had gotten friendly with Mike. They started eating lunch together at the store cafeteria on the ninth floor. Mike noticed that Rick would occasionally take a swig from a metal flask. He would offer Mike one every so often. Though tempted, he always declined. He thought however that the story would have a certain credibility if it were true. He could have been under the influence when he could have insulted a customer who he could not help pointing out had been grotesquely corpulent.

As he had realized, his father was working that Saturday. He therefore wasn't home when he got there around four o'clock in the afternoon, his and his father's usual arrival time around six o'clock aboard the 5:20 from Windsor station. They usually did not sit together on the train, mainly because the old man invariably sat with a neighbourhood man named Grant who also worked at Eaton's, upstairs in the furniture department. Besides, Mike's father and Mr. Grant preferred the sanctuary of the non-smoking car while Mike, though not exactly a habitual smoker, liked to occasionally light up on the train ride home. Mike's father did not appreciate his smoking but having been married for twenty years to a woman who smoked three packs of cigarettes a day, he had a little choice but to acquiesce with their unfortunate habit though he disapproved of it.

When he arrived home, he opened the front door to immediately observe his mother sitting at the kitchen table smoking a cigarette. She immediately turned toward him as he walked into the house. She had a disturbed look on her face as she stared at him through a cloud of exhaled Matinee Regular. She had the same look on her face anytime she caught him coming home after Mike's ridiculously early curfews, which was fairly often. He had expected her to be mildly suspicious anyway, coming home early from work on Saturday an obvious cue. But he recognized that her expression was different this time. It was more pronounced. It was obvious. She knew something, specifically that something unfortunate had happened during the day. He did not have to wait long to find out what.

She butted out her cigarette, took another out of the pack and fired it up with a silver butane lighter. He immediately recognized her tone. She knew. "Your father called me about an hour ago. His manager had just told him that you've been fired." She told a prolonged drag off her Matinee and seemed to take a moment to prepare herself. "He's as mad as hell. You've badly embarrassed your father with the people at work, especially with Mr. Larocque." Mike knew that Mr. Larocque was the manager of the notion department and therefore his father's manager. "I want you to sit down at the kitchen table here and wait for your father. I'm damn sure that he'll have something to say to you." Mike was mildly surprised. His mother seldom used any sort of profanity, no matter how serious the situation.

The two of them sat in silence. He watched his mother smoke several cigarettes while she started and then continued to prepare dinner: meatloaf, potatoes and canned peas. She allowed him to use the washroom and change out of his good clothes. He had sat there at the kitchen table for almost an hour until three passengers riding the 5:20 from Windsor Station disembarked at Valois Station. They included Mr. Grant, his father and an unidentified man man who was casually dressed and carrying a suitcase. It was a little after six o'clock and his father practically knocked the porch door down coming in the house. "Michael, I have to talk to you." His father always called him by his full name when he was in trouble with him. His was in the kitchen, both hands gripping the back of the chair on the other side of the kitchen table, staring at his son like he was about to hit him with something, just like the old days when corporal punishment was a constant possibility, not only at school but at home as well.

Father just stood there leaning over the chair, apparently considering his next move. Perhaps the transgression was too serious for a predictable reaction. While his father would usually resort to physical punishment for minor misdeeds, a penalty for major misconduct, such as getting fired from a job he basically engineered, may well have been beyond him. He then just sat down, deeply sighing, drawing in a deep breath and then exhaling, letting it out as his hands cradled his head. He muttered. "I just don't know what to say, I just don't." Another sigh and then he looked up at his wife. "What am I going to do, Ethel? What am going to do? Hell!" His mother's response was to start to ladle out dinner. His father just stared at his dinner and reached for the double scotch that his mother had surreptitiously poured for her husband before he had entered the kitchen. He took a drink and just sat there. He then began to eat. The anxiety warehousing in Mike's stomach started to evaporate. His mother quietly smiled. It was over, whatever it was.

His father hardly spoke to Mike for almost a month. His mother told him that he could help himself heal the rift with his father, who had been walking around the house with an irate look on his face, which worried both his wife, Mike and his two brothers, by getting another job. Further to a reference from his friend Pete, who told him that they were hiring, he started three weeks later at the Steinberg grocery store in the newly opened West Island Shopping Centre. In filling in the job application, for all purposes a formality it seemed, he neglected to record his recent position as a salesman in the men's wear department for the T. Eaton Co. He did, however, dutifully indicate his experience carrying golf clubs for members of the Beaconsfield Golf Club as previous employment.

THE EARLY YEARS
WORK ETHIC TRAINING II

H e started at the Steinberg grocery store on a Friday evening in November of 1966. His official job title was grocery clerk although pack boy would have been a more accurate description. He was to work Friday evenings and Saturdays packing groceries at the hourly wage of $1.10 per hour, which may have been the minimum wage at the time. He was given a punch clock card by his supervisor, a short stubby man with a small mustache. His name was Robert Tessier who then introduced him to the six cashiers for whom he would be packing groceries. All of them were women who looked to be in their thirties, wore a fair amount of make up and nail polish, and all but one of them were smoking cigarettes. Four of the six were wearing their hair in bee hive styles while the other two sported their hair in a style that used to be called a "flipped bob". Although not introduced, Mr. Tessier pointed out the store manager's name, Mr. Delorme. He was in the process of yelling at someone from the fruit and vegetable department when Mike reported that first evening.

That first Friday evening, his cashier was one of the bee

hive women. Her name was Monique and she had several extraordinary qualities. Not only was she supposedly the fastest cashier in the store, able to record the price of grocery products on the cash register with uncommon velocity but she could also smoke, chew gum and talk to the customers simultaneously. In addition, she could and often would berate not only her pack boys, which in his first few Friday nights was either Mike or an older guy named Maurice, as well as anybody, including the odd customer, who annoyed her. She also had a tawdry, alluring beauty that attracted practically every male in the store, including Mike. Aside from the hair and the make up, she wore, under a white apron, short skirts, low cut blouses and high heals, all of which precipitated obvious fantasies among the males in the store. During that first evening, Monique the cashier chastised him a couple of times for staring at her, allowing the groceries that he was supposed to be placing in paper bags and/or boxes, customers always having the choice, to pile up at the end of the conveyor belt, threatening occasionally to spill the purchases onto the floor. As Monique advised, if that happened, Mr. Delorme, who was always patrolling the front of the store, like he was with security as opposed to management, would have told him to immediately punch the clock and leave the premises. So it was that Mike usually had to scramble hard to catch up with the grocery packing. He noticed Monique smirk as he hastily tried to catch up with her passing items down the belt like cashiering was an Olympic sport.

Packing groceries on Saturday was a little less frantic than on Friday night, there being less urgency for shoppers on Saturday. Monique and three of the other full time cashiers did not work, their responsibilities being undertaken by part timers. There were two university students, an older woman who worked in accounting at the local hospital and another older woman who worked at the pharmacy across from Steinberg's in the West Island Shopping Centre. While the two older women showed a fair amount of speed in passing products through the cash and the university girls were acceptably efficient, none of the four were as nimble as the full time ladies, particularly Monique who wasn't but likely should have been paid triple what the weekend cashiers were. In addition, none of the four part time cashiers sported bee hive hair styles.

Unfortunately, at least as far as Mike was concerned, he packed groceries for one of the two older women, her name was Margaret and she had an annoying habit of engaging every customer in pointless conversation, even the men who looked embarrassed talking to her. Margaret might have been his mother's age, a possibility she confirmed by talking about her two sons in high school. When she didn't have a customer with whom to chitchat, a term she used to describe her socializing, she would talk to Mike. It was not an unpleasant experience although it certainty was repetitive: weather, business in the shopping centre, new housing developments in the area, her husband's health and her sons' educational careers being the substance of her conversations. Regarding the latter, she often wondered why her sons and Mike went to different high schools. Mike explained that his parents had been pious enough to send him to a Jesuit high school in the city. In contrast, her two boys went to a protestant high school less than a kilometer away from the shopping centre. Margaret also had the habit of teasing Mike about one of the university student cashiers about whom it was generally known Mike had developed a minor infatuation, his frequent staring at her sometimes so obvious that his co-workers often expressed surprise that neither Delorme nor Tessier had noticed. His co-workers also wondered whether the object of his fantasy had noticed. He didn't imagine that she hadn't.

The first time Mike was asked by Mr. Delorme to "take the door", an expression that was comparable to another term, "punch the clock", both intended to indicate that the person being asked was fired, was almost four months after he had started at Steinberg's. It was a Friday evening around 7:00 and Mike was working the bags for Monique who was flinging those grocery products down the conveyor with her usual speed and efficiency. He had packed three bags for a rather large woman who without warning decided that she would rather have her groceries packed in boxes rather than bags. Monique just shrugged with that imperious look of hers and told Mike to switch to boxes. After softly uttering a familiar profanity, he collected several medium size cardboard boxes from under the rollers at the front of the store, brought them back to his station and started to transfer the already bagged groceries into the boxes. He had filled at least one of the boxes when the large woman who had originally asked for the boxes announced that the boxes that Mike was using were too large and demanded that Mike use smaller boxes, claiming that the larger boxes were too heavy for her. Mike looked up from placing soup cans in one of the boxes, glanced at her with an exasperated look on his face, and offered her an observation "You look like you're big enough to carry those larger boxes.", an obvious reference to her weight.

The large woman shrieked, exclaiming to no one in particular. "Did you heard what this one just said?" She was pointing at Mike, standing in an accusatory posture, her hand and arm pointing straight at him. She had been loud enough to attract the attention of at least two dozen people, including several cashiers, several pack boys, and most of the remainder being customers. Mr. Delorme heard her as well and was now standing at the end of Mike's station. He beckoned to him. Mike took three or four steps over to Delorme who looked him straight in the face and gave him the dreaded order. Mike placed the soup can he had been holding on the conveyor, nodded toward Monique, dropped his apron and headed toward the back of the store where the punch clocks were. Mike found his card, inserted it in the punch clock, took his coat out of his locker, and headed out the front door of the grocery into the parking lot. Like his termination barely six months passed, he was now faced with concocting a story that his parents, particularly his father who he assumed still recalled, if not still incensed with his discharge from Eaton's, would somehow accept. For some reason, he wasn't as troubled as he had been with his previous experience of being asked to leave his place of employment. He didn't know why.

Again fortunately, his father was puttering around in his work shop, a distinct room in the unfinished part of the basement. The place was redolent of motor oil, gasoline and sawdust, all of which he would remember very clearly once he started working summer jobs in factories. Mike and his brothers were usually not permitted in their father's work shop, the only exception being those occasions when father would play barber and cut their hair, usually completing such an embarrassing job that they usually had to wear a cap until some of the hair their father had so clumsily removed grew back. Mike walked in the front door, hung up his coat and walked into living room where his mother was working on knitting another pair of socks, an avocation that she pursued with the same zeal as she smoked cigarettes. As much as the socks had ensured that their feet were warm, the boys, including Mike were not as appreciative as they should have been, especially at Christmas and on their birthdays when their expectations ran to less practical gifts. Mike stood on the edge of the living room, watching his mother knit. She looked up with an expectant look on her face, waiting for him to say something. He responded by telling her the whole story with understandable embellishments, including for example the suggestion that the large woman who made the complaint was well known throughout the West Island Shopping Centre as a difficult customer, a so-called "pain in the butt". His mother dropped her knitting needles, looked up and made an extraordinary claim, a surprising assertion that was to ultimately exonerate him with both Mr. Delorme and his mother. His father was never informed about the temporary loss of his job packing groceries. His mother, who was known to form the occasional critical opinions about people, told Mike that she knew the woman and that she agreed with the reputation that she had earned at the West Island Shopping Centre. "Yes, Michael, everybody knows that woman. Her name is Mrs. Nolan. She lives on Belmont Avenue. She has been annoying people for years with her silly complaints. She complains about everything, at the post office, in the train station, at school board meetings, and certainly in every store she's ever frequented. Everybody knows that." His mother paused for a moment and then offered him a promise. "Don't worry, Michael, I'll talk to your boss, what's his name?"

Mike, relieved and more impressed with his mother's talent for critical commentary about people than ever, answered hopefully. "You mean, Mr. Delorme?" She agreed. "I'll go see him maybe Monday morning at the store, when you know it isn't very busy, and I'll tell him about Ms. Nolan. Nobody should lose a job because of a complaint from that woman. Don't worry, you'll be back at Steinberg's before you know it." And then she added a final word of consolation. "And I won't tell your father and make sure you don't either." Mike smiled and agreed to keep it between the two of them. He just had to make sure that his father didn't notice that he didn't go to work the next day. After all, he didn't have his job back yet.

As his mother had promised, Mike was back at work at Steinberg's the following Friday evening. His mother told him that Mr. Delorme had agreed to give him his job back and to report to Mr. Tessier the next Friday evening at the usual time. Tessier, who welcomed him back to work by informing him that he was being transferred from packing groceries to placing packed groceries into cars for people who were too busy or too lazy to carry their own groceries out to the parking lot. He was now working in car orders. Tessier also advised Mike to keep out of Mrs. Delorme's sight which seemed like a sensible idea given the circumstances of his firing and then his rehiring.

He went to the rear of the store where his partner in placing groceries into the trunks of shoppers' cars was a guy named Jack, who didn't look like someone who Tessier or Delorme or anyone else, when he thought about it, would actually hire. He actually looked like he was addicted to something or other, physical features like long ratty hair, vacant eyes, and prematurely wrinkled face pretty well confirming the impression. He introduced himself to Jack who barked a greeting at him, lit a cigarette and correctly identified Mike as a "weekender", which almost sounded like an accusation. It did not take Jack long to demonstrate the benefits of working in car orders. They were basically without supervision, the work was basically sporadic, allowing for plenty of relaxation, and shoppers picking up car orders sometimes provided gratuities.

After a couple of months, working with the garage door open in the car order section took an unfortunate turn. Winter had arrived. It was cold outside and Mike and his new co- worker, another student ---- this one was named Brian, Jack having quit a month ago ---- were now battling the elements as they placed groceries in people's car trunks. Aside from the frigid weather, tips were down, shoppers unwilling it seemed to reach into their pockets with their car windows open. When there were no shoppers with their green car order tickets waiting for service, Brian and Mike would smoke cigarettes and sometimes a little weed, always supplied by Brian who said that he was planning to leave his parents' house once he managed to get enough money together, an ambition which seemed to Mike to be unattainable for a student making minimum wage for a twelve hour week and selling a little weed. The place also had the aroma of urine, the distance between the car order alcove and the employee washroom too inconvenient. They simply peed behind the rollers.

Mike worked the car order for the rest of the winter, making maybe $16-18 a week, maybe $14 which he received in cash in a pay envelope every week, plus $2-4 in gratuities from appreciative shoppers. Brian was pretty well useless after 7 PM on Friday evenings and 2 PM on Saturdays, his work habits becoming steadily worse, the most obvious example a growing tendency to throw rather than place the groceries into car trunks. When the weather improved, Mike discontinued the practice, assuming that shoppers were more likely to get out of their cars to complain if it wasn't so cold outside, that is if they noticed in the first place.

Mike retired from his duties at Steinberg's in the late spring without any further incident. He was informed by his mother that he would have to contribute to the tuition for his first year in college, which was due in several months. He had considered applying for a full time position at Steinberg's for the summer although he was told that there were few such positions available. Like many of his fellow students, he had applied for positions in the country pavilions, the restaurants and snack bars, and at the attached amusement park at the World's Fair in Montreal, otherwise known as Expo 67, without success, at least as far as he knew, his lack of bilingualism an obvious problem. On the other hand, however, his mother had managed to arrange a job interview for him at a small plastics factory out by the airport. While a possible job as a general labourer in a small factory was certainly not as glamorous as working at Expo 67, it likely paid more and was located not downtown but only several kilometers away from his home, easily reached by bicycle.

Appropriately dressed in a shirt, tie and jacket, one of his high school outfits, Mike went to see a man named Pete, whose brother Ray owed the factory. The owner brother had been nursed by his mother in the local hospital. She had told the man that her son was looking for a summer job in order to pay tuition for Loyola College. Pete showed his appreciation for her care by telling her that he had an opening for a summer student, last year's summer student having graduated to a better job elsewhere.

The shop itself, which was about the size of a gas station garage, held four plastic injection machines manufacturing plastic caps for bottles of a variety of products, salt shakers and the like. Mike and Pete both sat in a small disheveled office with a small desk and two chairs, a pin up girl calendar and an old adding machine which looked like it had not worked for years on the desk. Mike noticed that there was a punch clock installed on the wall outside his office. Next door was a much nicer office which apparently was shared by the company accountant, a remarkably well dressed man named Andre and the owner Ray, the brother and the recent discharge from the Lachine General Hospital. Both offices were situated in the front of the building underneath a barely legible sign which announced the Lawrence Plastics Company.

Pete the foreman asked Mike a couple of questions about his studies and his previous jobs. He then informed him, in a strangely casual voice, that he had been referred to him by his brother, who owned the place, and therefore was prepared to offer him a position tending to one of the plastic injection machines. He was to work for a guy named Roger, whose position he said was the "lead hand". He was to start in four days, on the first Monday of May 1967. He was to be paid $1.45 an hour for a forty hour week and his term would likely last until the end of the summer. His mother was delighted. She had immediately calculated that her son would earn more than $1,000 for the summer, easily more than enough she thought to pay for tuition, books and spending money. Mike, not certain that he would have enough to support his incidental spending, which had increased in the last few years, the maintenance of a succession of girlfriends the main justification.

It did not take him long to realize that working at the Lawrence Plastics Company was quite a bit different than working at Steinberg's, selling men's clothes at Eaton's, or carrying golf clubs at the Beaconsfield Golf Club. First of all, he was the only summer student working in the place, which immediately transformed him into a target of sarcastic and usually playful commentary from his new co-workers, all of whom seemed to have been found in central casting for working class heroes. Initially, the work seemed generally unpleasant, full of loud frightening noises, almost impenetrable smoke and shifting dust, bad odors, and barely recognizable shouting. He was, in short, working in a factory, a new experience for Mike. He thought of a nightmare in which he is sitting in his father's work shop with an oil soaked rag over his mouth, his hair clippers turned on high ringing in both ears, sawdust being thrown in his face and a bunch of guys screaming profanity laden insults at each other, even though they didn't.

That first day on the job, the first Monday in May 1967, Mike was introduced to Roger, the "lead hand" who was to be his supervisor. He immediately recognized him from somewhere. It took Mike maybe five minutes to identify that somewhere. It was a miraculous coincidence when he thought about it. Roger had been one of the two older guys who played cards all day sitting on wooden boxes at the top of the stairs to the caddy shop at the Beaconsfield Golf Club. Surprisingly, while he could not have expected it, Roger actually recognized him when he said that he had remembered him from the caddy shop at the Beaconsfield Golf Club, laughingly referring to him as "the guy with that stupid straw hat", a reference to that comical cap that his mother had insisted he wear to the golf course. Mike had found a mentor and he had not been on the job for more than five minutes.

Ray then introduced him to the others working on the floor on the day shift: an older man named Guy, the company machinist and die maker who was occasionally assisted by Roger who later explained that his ambition was to be certified as a die maker; a tall quiet man named Jean Paul who ensured that the four injection machines were properly maintained; a laborer named Pierre, who everyone teased and derided because of his weight and generally dull demeanor; and three middle aged men who tended to the operation of the machines. Unlike Mike, however, who also was responsible for the input and output of the machines, the three middle aged men also worked for the fire station across the street from the factory. Apparently and understandably Mike concluded, their responsibilities to the fire station took precedence over the responsibilities to Lawrence Plastics. Accordingly, if called away by the fire station, their duties at Lawrence Plastics were suspended, machines either shut down or managed by someone else. As Roger was to observe with considerable admiration, if not envy, that was how the three were able to drive such nice automobiles, the advantage of receiving wages from two full time positions self evident. Roger sometimes also wondered whether any of them had more than one wife. At first, Mike had assumed that he was being facetious but after a month or so, he became to question that opinion.

Mike found his duties, while uncomfortable, almost absurdly simple, consisting mainly of heating raw material in the form of plastic pellets into a liquid which is then injected through molded dies to form plastic bottle caps. Mike was not required to know anything about the injection process, however efficient an engineering marvel it was, his duties limited to pouring pellets into the hopper at front end of the machine and removing the finished bottle caps at the other. He was also required to ensure that the injection mechanism did not jam, a misfortune that could delay production by as much as a day, not to mention the inevitable clean up of the shop floor. Still, the machine noises, the smoke, the dirt, the smells and the incomprehensible shouting made the 8 AM to 4:30 PM daily grind tiresome, if not miserable, even at the handsome wage of $1.45 an hour. After five weeks of working at Lawrence Plastics, he had confirmation of his preference for school rather than work, the soon to be longstanding slogan "It sure beats working." began to take the form of a sort of mantra. He had no doubt.

The only bright spot in working that summer, the first time he had worked a forty hour week just like an adult, if there was in fact a bright spot, was the time he spent socializing with Roger, supposedly his supervisor but more like his mentor, if not his friend. He not only instructed him on the intricacies of plastic injection production, which took him about ten minutes, but also shared with him his everyday life, much of which was well beyond his own. Although only three or four years the elder, Roger seemed to have had a variety of experiences Mike had not shared and was not likely to share, unless his life was to take a sudden turn from its current course. Roger was obviously a working class guy, street smart but not educated, having survived school until grade eight. He reminded Mike of an older guy with whom he had worked at Eaton's the previous summer. Either him or one of the older guys who found themselves still attending elementary school well into their teens. Regarding the latter, Roger could easily pass for Rick McPhee, the motorcycle driving guy with brilliantine hair who had shared his grade six class with Mike six or seven years ago.

Roger did not, however, have a motorcycle. He drove a new Dodge Challenger, an impressive looking automobile painted red with black racing stripes. Mike was even more impressed when he met Roger's girlfriend, an extremely attractive blonde girl who worked in a gentleman's club in Lachine, which was where Roger first made her acquaintance. Her name was Giselle. Mike met her when Roger dropped by the factory on a day off specifically to introduce her. She looked to be around Mike's age and was surprisingly friendly, at least to Mike who usually assumed that woman who looked like Giselle were never particularly friendly, at least not to guys who did not drive impressive looking automobiles. Despite his repeated invitations, Mike never accompanied Roger to the strip club at which Giselle danced. To Mike, Giselle had developed a mystique. It was like, in fact it likely was, an adolescent crush. He did not tell Roger but Mike thought he knew anyway.

Things changed in August. He had only a little more than two weeks left before his stint at Lawrence Plastics would end. One evening shift, which was unusual not only for Roger but for Mike as well, both working evenings only once every six weeks, events conspired to produce a curious and unfortunate result. Roger, who was commonly regarded as a valued employee, particularly by the owner and his brother the foreman, often took advantage of his reputation to engage in foolishness. Fact was that when Roger wasn't performing his duties as the "lead hand" and assistant die maker, he was a known smart aleck, often inflicting all sorts of tricks on his co-workers, things like removing the tires from the cars of co-workers, leaving dog excrement in lockers, leaving pictures of sandwiches instead of actual sandwiches in the lunch boxes of his co-workers, and throwing cold water on guys in the showers. Ray sometimes asked Roger to discontinue his antics but not often, admitting to himself that they were sometimes entertaining. Mike was not unfamiliar with such hi jinks, having seen different examples in his previous positions, examples including such trickery as placing golf balls in soup in the dinner room of the golf club, jamming cash register drawers in the grocery store, or disrobing the mannequins in a department store.

During this particular evening shift, as they were enjoying their dinner, a pizza delivered by a place called Mello's, Roger noticed the pudgy, dull witted Pierre open the door to the factory washroom, which sat in the middle of the shop floor, a porcelain toilet and sink surrounded by plywood walls. Roger pointed out that Pierre was carrying a copy of *Allo Police*, a tabloid which featured, in addition to crime reports and lurid stories about local celebrities, pictures of naked women. Roger made an observation. "You know why he's going into there, don't you?" He then made an obscene up and down motion with his right hand. "It's time for him to beat the meat, if you know what I mean." Then he laughed. He waited for Pierre to close the door to the makeshift washroom and then made a proposal. "Hey, let's have some fun." Mike immediately knew that Roger had some sort of mischievous prank in mind.

Mike was only able to mumble "Okay." He was a bit nervous, always concerned that he could somehow be associated with the nonsense and then get into trouble with the Ray or even worse, his brother. Roger then stood up, went over to and started the fork lift truck. He moved it slowly toward the washroom, brought the forks down and slid them under the bottom of its back wall. With the noise of the machines going, there being two running on the evening shift, Roger's maneuvers could not be heard, presumably by three people on the floor, including Pierre. Roger lifted the back wall off the floor and then pulled the entire structure off its moorings. As intended, Pierre was suddenly exposed, sitting on the toilet, his trousers and underwear around his ankles and a copy of *Allo Police* quickly and conveniently positioned across his genitals, which both Roger and Mike assumed had been in a state of arousal. Pierre let out something akin to a scream and tried to pull up his pants. While Pierre struggled with his pants and his mortification, Roger began to laugh. He continued to laugh as Pierre, his face a pale crimson, ran toward the locker room as he pulled up his pants, now crying. Roger looked at Mike, still laughing and shrugged. He then backed the fork lift up and placed the washroom walls back on its moorings. He then parked the fork lift and disembarked. They both had a cigarette and went back to work. Neither of them saw Pierre for the rest of the evening shift.

When Mike arrived for the evening shift the next day, he was asked to report to Ray's office where he found both he and his brother waiting. Since both chairs in the office were occupied, Mike nervously stood by the door, sensing that the conference may have something to do with the previous evening's proceedings. He was reminded of those unfortunate occasions when he was sent to the principal's office. Not surprisingly, Pete Lawrence did the talking. Ray was smoking a cigarette. He looked as nervous as Mike was. Lawrence looked straight at him and, in a firm voice, spoke to him. "Mike, we have to talk to you. We're facing a situation here in the shop, a bad situation" Mike wished he could sit down. He felt faint. "I understand that you and Roger were involved in an incident last night with Pierre, an incident that we have to take seriously." Mike felt fainter still. He was in trouble. He knew it. "I don't know if you know that Pierre is, in a way, a special person." The brothers looked at Mike, hopefully, as if they wouldn't have to explain anything to him. But they did. "Well, Mike, he is a little handicapped, I mean mentally handicapped, a little slow you'll understand. He has been working here for years." Mike nodded, now understanding why Pierre's duties in the shop seemed so limited. He was the shop's custodian, basically a janitor who occasionally pushed a broom around the place and looked confused much of the time. "I know you guys tease him all the time. Ray and I don't like to see you doing that but as long as things don't go too far, we don't say anything."

There was a slight delay and then Mr. Lawrence continued. "Well, his mother, who Ray and I have known for years, called me early this morning and told me that Pierre was basically out of control, so upset that she and her husband, who by the way worked here some time ago, had to take him to emergency late last night, where they had to sedate the poor kid. She also told him that Pierre wouldn't be coming back, at least not for a while." Mike now wanted to faint. Either that or run out of the room. Pete Lawrence then lowered his voice somewhat and took on an even more serious tone, as if that were even possible given the gravity of what he had just told him. "I know that you and Roger tormented that poor boy terribly last night, scaring him while he was on the toilet for god's sake." Pete paused for a moment, put his hand in his hands and looked up. "Roger told us the whole story. I spoke to him on the telephone this morning. I told him that I would have to suspend him for a couple of days."

Bill then stood up, came out from behind the desk, and approached Mike to apparently shake his hand. Ray also stood up. "I'm sorry, Mike, but I'm going to have to let you go. I'm promised Pierre's parents that there would be consequences for what you guys did to their poor son last night. I think a couple of days for Roger and your termination will satisfy them. You'll understand that I can't fire Roger. He's been with us too long and he's far too valuable an employee. Besides, you only have two weeks left anyway." He offered Mike his hand. Mike shook it. He shook Ray's hand as well. He turned to leave the office to punch out for the final time. Ray then spoke for the first time during their meeting. "Look, we'll mail you your final cheque in a week or so. And we won't call your parents. You should tell them that we're given you a two week vacation."

And that was that for his summer in the employ of the Lawrence Plastics Company.

THE EARLY YEARS
WORK ETHIC TRAINING III

Mike's mother seemed to accept the explanation of his shortened summer job at the Lawrence Plastics Company. She offered to call Mr. Lawrence to thank him for offering him the job in the first place. Mike was immediately worried that Lawrence would spill the beans about the circumstances leading to the premature termination of his job. On the other hand, Mike assumed that if his mother called Mr. Lawrence, he would provide him with an appropriate explanation. In any event, his mother never got around to calling Mr. Lawrence while his father, who often did not seem aware of Mike's job, only that he had one, did not seem surprised to see Mike sleeping in on the weekdays, at least for the three weeks before school started in the second week of September.

Once Mike received his final cheque, by mail as promised, he began to formulate his financial plans for the coming school year. He would pay the tuition and books for his first year of college. It was a more than $600. It would be the first time he had ever filled in and signed a personal cheque. It was supplied to him by the Bank of Montreal on Donegani Avenue, a bank in which he had an account since he had started carrying golf clubs for players at the Beaconsfield Golf Club. It did not take him long to realize that he would run out of spending money by Christmas. After that, he would need income to satisfy his financial needs, which were concentrated on things like smokes, fries and cokes, his girlfriend, if he had one, and draft beer at the selected taverns, basically places which would serve anyone of any age, which was a pretty common practice in Montreal anyway. He immediately thought of returning to Steinberg's grocery store at the West Island Shopping Centre, probably after Christmas when his funds would run out. He was confident that Steinberg's would rehire him, experience and general dependability he thought more important than an occasional lapse in judgment, his temporary termination the previous spring hopefully overlooked or forgotten. He could wait.

His first semester at college was hardly exemplary. He went to maybe half his classes, the pursuit of a pedestrian arts degree hardly requiring much of an effort. In addition, he was less than fully attentive during many of the classes to which he did show up, the influence of either weed, liquor or the occasional hallucinogen responsible most of the time. Oddly enough, he was seldom asked to leave any of those classes, simply going to sleep apparently not disruptive enough to merit ejection. In fact, the only occasions was when he had the temerity to ask a question in class, usually and predictably something that made no sense. He had a daily routine that would inevitably lead to misbehavior. He got out of bed well after both his father and mother had left for work and his two brothers had left for school. He had nothing for breakfast except a few cigarettes and a couple of scotches if available from his parents' liquor cabinet. He then would walk down to get the 10:40 CP train to Montreal West, walk from the station to the campus of Loyola College and head straight to a student lounge on the top floor of the Administration Building, where he could usually find someone he knew. Sometimes, someone would have some weed. And sometimes, he'd join them in a couple of tokes and then he was off to one of the two student cafeterias. His first class, at least for three days of the week, was scheduled for 12:40 PM, the other two days started at 10:00 AM, that is if he bothered attending those classes at all.

Regarding his future work intentions, his plan was to reapply at Steinberg's just before Christmas in order to ensure that he could start another weekend stint after Christmas. But that was changed when his date for the high school graduation dance the previous June, a socially active, if not wanton girl named Alicia whose propensity for alcohol would prove legendary, telephoned him sometime in November. He immediately recalled their date for the graduation dance. It has not gone well for either of them, ending as it had with a drunken Alicia, her dress disheveled and her corsage long gone, getting out of a cab at 6:15 in the morning without any sort of gesture or comment. He figured that he would never see her again. That prognostication, however, turned out to be wrong. He saw her at the Fairview Shopping Centre in Pointe Claire maybe two months later. She was handing out sales fliers in the front of the Simpson's department store. He walked, or at least he tried to walk by her without being noticed, his memory of their graduation night fiasco current enough for him to avoid her. But she did not seem to share his sentiments about that night. She went out of her way to acknowledge him as he walked past her, waving at him and then gracing him with one of her killer expressions, more a pout than a smile, a look that implied something that he did not really understand, at least not at his age. He pretended that he had not seen her, walking past her without acknowledging her. She looked confused for a moment and then went back to distributing fliers. He regretted his reaction almost immediately and then thought about it for the rest of the summer. He sincerely doubted that she thought about it at all.

It was towards the end of November when Alicia telephoned Mike. It was around nine o'clock on a Wednesday evening. He had been enjoying a cigarette while watching television in the basement playroom. His mother, who for unknown reasons was usually suspicious about any call that anyone in the house received after dinner, called down to him, announcing in a predictably stern tone that some girl was on the line for him. He put out his cigarette and ran up the stairs like the house was about to catch fire. He of course was shocked. He was not in the habit of receiving telephoning calls from girls, particularly if he could not think of any reason to have expected one, a call from the occasional steady girlfriend being the only such case. His mother, who was gripping the telephone receiver like someone was able to grab it from her, handed it to Mike almost reluctantly.

"Were you expecting a call from some girl?" she asked, an accusatory look on her face augmented by the cigarette between her teeth. He could tell that she didn't require or even care about an answer. He took the receiver from his mother, hurriedly retreated to the vestibule and then closed the door. It was his habit to hide there anytime he either made a call to or, in exceptional circumstances, received a call from a girl. His mother, who barely tolerated the practice, called the vestibule the confessional anytime Mike went in there to keep his telephone calls confidential.

She always made him feel guilty about any relationship he managed to have with a girl. He never really knew the reason for her disapproval.

The girl turned out to be Alicia, a startling development given that, aside from a wave at a shopping centre, he had not communicated with her in any way since their unfortunate graduation night date. She did not seem in the least way to be shy about her call. After some introductory banter during which she told him, without elaboration, that she had been thinking about him recently, she casually asked if he had a friend who could be convinced to double date with the two of them and a friend of hers. She sounded like she was asking him for a cigarette, the question was that perfunctory, that informal. Mike was mesmerized for a moment, thinking that he may be imagining the call.

"Sure, sure, okay.", nervous enthusiasm coming through the telephone that was difficult to hear. And he made a quick recovery and a suggestion. "I could ask my friend Steve"., a reference to one of his classmates, one of two good friends who, along with their dates, had joined Alicia and Mike for dinner prior to the graduation dance the past June. Mike could hear Alicia quietly chuckle on the other end of the telephone.

"What about his date for the evening? I forget her name." she asked.

"Her name was Joyce. They weren't steadies or anything." Mike replied.

"You mean he would be willing?" Alicia observed and chuckled again.

Mike answered, his enthusiasm unwavering. "I'm pretty sure he would be. In fact, I'm positive." Another chuckle from Alicia. She had been positive about his response before she had dialed his number. Then Mike asked about their planned date. "What's her name, I mean your friend's name?"

"Cathy. Her name is Cathy." And then she added a qualifying request, if not a requirement. "Do either of you have a car?" They had taken taxis on their graduation dance date.

"Actually Steve has a car, his own car." Mike said. It was a used Volkswagen. A week later, the four of them were sitting at a table in a local place called the Edgewater, situated on the shore of Lake St Louis, a dinner club on the ground floor with a nightclub in the basement. The club featured live bands on the weekends and did not seem to mind serving minors. Mike and Steve, the latter not requiring much convincing to agree to the double date proposal, were surprised to see that both Alicia and Cathy appeared to know most of the waiters in the place. They ordered drinks, Alicia having an obvious affinity for Zombies, a cocktail that required several kinds of rum, an ounce of brandy, and fruit juices at a cost of $4.50 a glass. Mike, Steve and Cathy were content with beer. They did a fair amount of dancing, Mike's intention being that the more often she was on the dance floor, the less she was drinking. Still, that first evening cost him almost $20.00, well beyond his usual budget for the week. In fact, he had instantly and anxiously calculated that one more evening with Alicia, with or without Steve and Cathy, would bankrupt him, requiring him to find a source of income. For days after their date, a date which ended with a limited make out session in the back seat of Steve's car while the latter struggled in the front seat with Cathy, Mike was obsessed with his financial situation.

On that point, regardless of their romantic misadventures of that first date, all four of them agreed that there would be a second date, the next Saturday evening night at the

Edgewater. Steve appeared to be more enthused than Mike, which seemed a trifle curious. Three days later, he arranged to meet Steve for cokes and fries in the student cafeteria out by the hockey arena. In discussing their date for the coming Saturday, Mike mentioned his need for cash, telling Steve that he only had enough money to underwrite one more date with Alicia. Steve had no such difficulty, his father not only subsidizied his expenses with a weekly allowance but also provided ng him with a part time job working at his accounting firm. In other words, Steve had no financial problems. He did, however, have a suggestion.

"Look, it's, what, five weeks until Christmas. Check down at the Post Office, they always hire for Christmas. It would be a government job, good money, and I think they'll hire almost anyone."

Mike looked at Steve with this contemplative look on his face. A temp job at the Post Office until Christmas would fit his plans, his plans now that a weekly date seemed to be part of them. And then, he could hopefully return to Steinberg's for weekend work after Christmas, his application already filed there. "Hey, that's a pretty good idea. I should apply, shouldn't I?"

"Yeah, you should."

Three days later, it was a Monday afternoon, Mike was standing in the sorting room of the main postal station on Donegani Avenue, waiting with maybe other recently hired recruits to start their shifts. He was to work four hours an evening three days (Tuesday, Wednesday and Friday) a week for the next four weeks, until the Friday before Christmas, specifically in the sorting room. Mike and seven other guys, all of whom would turn out to be students, would be making $3.25 an hour, more than double they would be paid if they weren't occupying a union job. Their duties as inside postal workers, more accurately called temporary mail sorting clerks, were simple. The mail collected from the mail boxes in the area would arrive in bags and then dumped in a series of bins. The sorting clerks, of which Mike was one, would then take mail out of the bins and place each piece of mail in appropriate boxes on the wall, which were arranged by street address. Mike was responsible for the addresses on five neighbourhood streets, including surprisingly enough his own.

That first evening, Mike and the other guys on the evening shift noticed some rather curious behavior from the guys on the day shift. They were the permanent employees, a half dozen men ranging in age from their twenties to middle aged. The evening guys, who were all in their late teens, usually showed up for work about fifteen or twenty minutes before their shift was able to begin. They would find the day shift guys sitting around the sorting room smoking and discussing predictable topics, invariably involving women and complaining about their jobs which seemed, at least to Mike, almost absurdly easy. Then, as soon as the shift changed, as soon as four o'clock in the afternoon rolled around, the day shift guys would suddenly spring into action, their task to finish the batches of mail that had accumulated over the past hour or so. The evening shift boys would have to wait until the day shift boys finished the sorting for the day. After several days on the job, one of Mike's evening shift co-workers mustered the temerity to ask one of the day shift guys for an explanation. A guy named Guy told him that in order to ensure overtime, which according to their union contract was a minimum of four hours, they would have to allow the mail to pile up. The evening shift guys began to think that the day shift guys were a lot smarter than they seemed. Some of them began to wonder about pursuing careers in the post office, questioning the utility of going to college. One even said that he had asked the evening shift supervisor, a disagreeable guy named Roger Monfils, for a job application.

After working the evening shift for several weeks, their understandable cynicism about sorting mail had grown almost terminal. They worked so efficiently that Monfils had to constantly tell them to slow down, an extraordinary request thought the dutiful clerks. He was particularly worried that the day shift guys would get the wrong idea, their comparative sloth in sorting mail easily exposed to managers. The evening guys often spent the last hour of their shifts not working at all, playing card games, mainly Hearts and an unfamiliar game, at least to Mike, called Euchre. They would sometimes invent games, throwing letters into the address boxes a particular favorite.

His weekly wages for his three evenings of work amounted to about $35.00 a week, which was more than enough to underwrite his weekly festivities at the Edgewater with Alicia, who everyone had started calling "Boozeanna", a clever reference to her obvious ability to consume alcohol. He realized, however, that his finances would take a significant hit after his temporary stint at the post office expired just before Christmas, his planned return to packing groceries at Steinberg's after the holidays would pay him less than half the amount he was earning at the post office. His plans got less optimistic, however, when he and three of evening shift colleagues were fired by Mr. Monfils after he had received reports of their nonsensical pursuits in the mail sorting room. Understandably, while adolescent foolishness like pitching letters at the address boxes was overlooked by Monfils, of which he had informed more than once, defacing the mail by writing ridiculous slogans and placing crude drawings on letters before they were placed in the appropriate address boxes was a serious enough offense for Monfils to fire the offenders. They thought that Monfils might involve the police. Though they were worried about the possibility for a couple of weeks or so, they were fortunate that Monfils never did involve any other authority.

Mike and the other three miscreants lost pay for only three evenings due to their dismissal from their temp jobs at the post office. As planned, Mike returned to his weekend position packing groceries at Steinberg's in January, by which time Boozeanna had ended their regular Saturday night arrangement at the Edgewater. His financial position was therefore improved. It was incidental that Alicia's friend Cathy had a week earlier stopped accompanying his friend Steve on those Saturday nights. Almost immediately, Mike had thought that the fact that they no longer had access to transportation by Steve may have had something to do with his breakup from Alicia. The two of them had made one appearance at the Edgewater without Steve and Cathy. They had to use cabs and there was no making out in the back seat or anywhere else.

THE EARLY YEARS
WORK ETHIC TRAINING IV

Mike returned to Steinberg's after that Christmas, back on grocery packing duty on Friday evenings and all day Saturday. For the next four months, he worked the twelve hours a week without incident, no attention from either Mr. Tessier or Mr. Delorme, industriously placing groceries into paper bags or cardboard boxes without comment or complaint. He wasn't offered, nor did he ever consider asking for another assignment, the fruit and vegetable and meat departments having had part time openings over the winter. Regarding events in the former, Delorme had fired two guys, a couple of numb skulls who were rumored to have been caught throwing pieces of fruit at each other back in the warehouse. The real story, at least according to head cashier Monique, was that they had allowed some bruised fruit to have been placed on display. As for the meat department, the idea of handling cold meat frightened Mike for some reason. He didn't know why there was an opening in the meat department. Otherwise, his most recent and final stint at Steinberg's was remarkably tranquil, a raise of 25 cents an hour an added benefit.

As the end of the school year approached, he had begun to seek another summer job, filing in applications at various firms in the Pointe Claire industrial park as well as stores in the West Island Shopping Centre. As he trudged from one personnel office to another, he replayed the events leading to his premature departure from Lawrence Plastics the previous summer. He thought that maybe if he had not been cashiered from Lawrence, he could have relied on Mr. Lawrence to provide him with a summer job for the next four years, relieving him of his annual summer job search anxieties. Over those past few weeks, his mother occasionally asked Mike why he didn't just contact Mr. Lawrence. He told her that Lawrence wasn't hiring anybody for the summer anyway, claiming that the company had lost a contract to a competitor in the east end of Montreal. Although she expressed some sympathy for her son's plight, it did not change his situation. He needed a summer job.

It took another three weeks but he did manage to get hired on as a summer student at a company which assembled chainsaws and other products. The company, which was called Ferry Industries, had a factory out by the Trans Canada highway in the Pointe Claire Industrial Park, a nexus of manufacturing facilities, plants, factories, workshops, mills, warehouses and empty yards of unknown purpose. He somehow had impressed the personnel director of Ferry, an elfin little man with a bad complexion whose name was Alex Morrisette, enough for him to hire Mike as a machine operator for the summer at $1.75 per hour. Before he was officially offered the job, Mr. Morrisette walked Mike into the plant and introduced him to several of the plant superiors, all of whom unnerved him in one way or another. In charge of plant production was a frightening looking man in a nicotine stained black suit. He wore sun glasses inside the plant and was constantly smoking unfiltered cigarettes. His name was Ray Arbec. Mike must have heard the plant public address system calling him to the office at least three times during his twenty minute tour. He was also introduced to four other presumed supervisors: a tall German gentleman named Ernest Gerhard who was the foreman of the press room and to whom Mike was to ultimately report; an apparently self-effacing man named Roger Proulx, who ran the annealing and painting room; a short, squat, spectacularly muscular man named Andrew who was apparently the only guy who operated the sheet cutter; and a fat curmudgeonly guy known as Charlie Balfour, the plant carpenter. Regarding the latter individual, Mike was to later find out that fat Charlie wasn't the only irascible individual that worked in Ferry Industries.

Mike was to start on the second Monday of May, 1968. His mother prepared a bag lunch for him, something she had not done since he was in his first year of high school. He left the house at 7:15 AM and pedaled his three speed to the Ferry, arriving at 7:45 AM to report for 8 AM. He was met by personnel director Morrisette who gave him a card for the punch clock, escorted him to the plant locker room, where he deposited his bag lunch into his locker, changed into an industrial green pant and shirt outfit, put on his recently purchased work boots, and then accompanied him to the chainsaw assembly section where he was introduced to Gerhard's lead hand Maurice, a.k.a. Moe Boivin. After some understandably abbreviated pleasantries, Moe brought Mike over to the one of punch press machines, a cast iron behemoth that he immediately noted was built in Manchester, England in the last decade of the previous century. Boivin somehow had noticed that Mike had identified the machine's origins, informing him that this particular Ferry plant happened to have collected a majority of its machinery from old factories that had gone bankrupt in the old country, namely England.

There were two other punch presses of similar vintage in the room, one on either side of Mike's machine. The machine was operated by a foot pedal circulating a flywheel drive which then forced a metal die down to punch or stamp a hole in a piece of metal. The machine on the left was operated by a tall, leathery faced man who looked like he might have had or still had a drinking problem. To the right was another summer student who would let out a yelp every time his punch press malfunctioned, a double strike of the die being the cause. Lead hand Boivin was kind enough to caution Mike about what he called "a minor problem". Mike disagreed with Boivin's description of the problem, observing that the malfunction was more than "a minor problem" but actually posed a danger to whoever was operating that specific press. He was glad, however, that his fellow student to his right was operating the defective push press and not him. In addition, after only a half a day, Mike first heard him --- his name was Harvey --- complain not so much about the machine but the fact that they were being unfairly exploited by "the capitalist system", an observation that, while he thought probably accurate, was still annoying. As soon as Mike become acquainted with Harvey, he constantly advised him to limit, if not discontinue his complaints about the exploitative capitalist system.

About Mike's comments to him about "a minor problem", Boivin just shrugged and commented. "You just have to be careful, that's all. Otherwise, you could lose your fingers.", expressing that last observation as if the advice was obvious. Mike operated the punch press machine for almost a month, during which time he managed to strike up friendships with three other summer students that Ferry Industries had hired during the summer of 1968. There was Harvey of course, who continued to complain about capitalism and exploitation, a gawky, lumbering guy named Tim who liked to flash the peace sign every chance he got, and a guy named Paul who often ran into trouble with Roger Proulx of annealing room fame for asking the latter not to smoke over the tubs of flammable chemicals. Mike and Paul often had lunch together, either out in the yard of the plant or, if they had to, in the plant canteen.

That first summer working at Ferry, Mike was surprised when he was witness to two incidents that easily could have been classified as industrial accidents. Surprisingly, during the four months he spent the previous summer working at the Lawrence Plastics Company, there were no mishaps of any disastrous consequence, unless of course if you counted the lavatory prank played on the slow witted Pierre, which ultimately led to Mike's termination. Otherwise, there was little, if any event that could have been qualified as anything comparable to the industrial accidents that Mike observed at Ferry Industry. In one of the events, a man named Rene, who was assigned to the paint shop, fell into a vat of primer and almost drowned. It was reported that Rene was submerged for a minute or so, long enough for him to be sent to the hospital. The other event was far more serious. In fact, it resulted in a fatality.

Mike didn't know his name. In fact, he thought that most people, except officials in the personnel department, probably didn't know his name either. He was a tall, sinewy character possibly in his forties although he could easily have been much older. He had the face of a statue, a countenance that seldom expressed any sort of emotion. He seldom spoke to anyone, basic nodding and shrugging his basic reactions to almost everything, including basic greetings from his colleagues or instructions from the boss. His assignment was that of a grinder, removing metal particles from the handlebars of the chainsaws assembled by Ferry Industries. He accomplished this task by standing behind a rotating stone wheel. It was a profoundly monotonous job, a tedious task that most of his associates usually avoided if they could.

Mike had been working his normal duties at one of the punch press machines, transforming blank steel pellets into handlebar plugs, when it happened. While he did not witness the poor, nameless man's death, Mike did observe some of the physical remnants of the deadly accident. Right in front of his station was a steel partition that separated him from the remainder of the press section. Just after a crowd of the man's co-workers crowded around him just after the accident happened, Mike noticed, as did a few members of the crowd, that there were fragments of skin and blood spattered all over the partition. This prompted foreman Gerhard to whisper something to his lead hand Boivin and immediately headed for the office of plant supervisor Arbec who would normally be on the plant floor but must have been struggling with his paperwork. Within five minutes, Arbec was standing in front of the incident, shaking his head and presumably discussing the unfortunate implications that the death of Mr. Misura, Mike had overheard the name of the previously nameless man as the crowd continued to congregate, would have for Ferry Industries. It was apparent that the possibility of a legal suit figured prominently in Arbec's concerns. Mike also overheard another name, a Mr. Wiseman, who happened to be the general director of

Ferry Industries. Like most, if not all of the employees of Ferry Industries, Mike only knew Wiseman by name, never having seen him. Once the two attendants departed after loading the now faceless Mr. Misura into an ambulance which had been backed into the plant garage, two of the plant's janitorial staff arrived to clean up the mess left by the accident. Not surprisingly, there was a new man behind the grinder within a day. The handlebars were piling up.

Over the next several weeks, there was a lot of discussion of previous accidents that had occurred in the plant. It was rumoured that two workers were seriously injured in the past month, one with the loss of three fingers while the other suffered a serious gash on his hand. Those two incidents were relatively trivial compared to a much more significant mishap which had resulted in the death of a man who was unfortunate to have his long hair caught in the fly wheel of an old fashioned punch press, that last winter. Now and then, press room lead hand Boivin liked to frighten one of his charges by describing in considerable detail the grisly accident that befell the worker with the long hair. And then there was the case of Mr. Misura.

The next summer, he was assigned the position as the assistant to the plant carpenter for Ferry Industries, Charlie Balfour. Charlie worked for Ferry since he was sixteen years old when the plant was located in Montreal East and he was the second assistant to the then plant carpenter whose name was Gendron. It was now thirty years later. He now weighed upwards of three hundred pounds, a cherub like character, usually attired in an dirty pair of denim coveralls that looked like they hadn't been laundered in twenty years.

He smoked unfiltered cigarettes, and wore bifocal glasses held together with Scotch Tape. In addition, he was close to completely deaf, making conversations with him difficult. He seldom made sense even when he did engage in any sort of discussion. On the other hand, he was still regarded as an competent carpenter even though he sometimes had trouble nailing two boards together, particularly after lunch when he washed down his baloney sandwiches with passes from a metal flask.

Initially, Mike was pleased with the position, thinking that it would be less repetitive, if not less labour intensive than last summer's jobs until he was told that working for Charlie Balfour, was rumoured to be like sharing responsibilities with an badly behaved eight year old. Sure, he had a number of unusual habits. He had a makeshift office in the back of the building where he would sit on a wooden box, sometimes without his pants, smoke ceaselessly, taking frequent passes at either large bottles of homemade beer or his flask, read men's magazines, and talk endlessly, regardless of whether anyone was listening to him. So it was that Mike was told by Mr. Gerhard, who was normally in charge of Charlie Balfour, that he should watch Charlie carefully. Aside from his habits, which were understandably unorthodox, Mike didn't realize the importance of Gerhard's advice until, three weeks into his tenure with the carpenter, Charlie told him to begin helping him build bird houses which he then told Mike he intended to install on the plant's roof. In addition, Charlie was extremely protective about his tools, often criticizing Mike or anyone else for that matter for even touching any of them, let alone using any of them. In fact, Mike almost lost his position as Charlie's assistant when the latter accused him of stealing his favorite hammer. It was an entirely false accusation but Charlie never recanted. Mr. Gerhard said that was normal.

There was therefore little to commend Mike's second summer working at Ferry. Aside from his struggles with Charlie, there were a couple of episodes that he could relate to college classmates interested in working class hero stuff. Episode one. Most of the workers, at least the full timers, brought their lunches to work in metal lunch containers that they usually kept in their lockers. For reasons that Mike never understood, one of the blue collars, whose name he eventually learned was Pierre Lemaire, accused Mike of accidentally forcing him to drop his lunch box, a mishap which resulted in breaking his thermos. For the next several weeks, there was talk around the factory that Lemaire, who worked in the annealing room and had a reputation for being somewhat of a tough guy, was thinking of exacting some sort of retribution from Mike for breaking his thermos. Mike was understandably alarmed by the possibility and took care to avoid Lemaire which was not that difficult since the annealing room was at the far end of the plant. The only place that could present a problem was the locker room itself where Lemaire could supposedly teach him a lesson. Mike spent at least two weeks not only avoiding Lemaire but the locker room as well. His anxiety eventually faded as Lemaire apparently forgot about the incident.

The other episode involved a man who worked in shipping. His name was Kubicek. He was well known around the plant for smoking Turkish cigarettes and driving an old British compact car, something called a Vauxhall. Kubicek used his car to ferry any coworker anywhere if they were willing to pay him. In other words, Kubicek operated an "off the books" taxicab. After one Friday after work, Mike and another summer employee named Dennis engaged Mr. Kubicek to drive them downtown, where the two of them planned to meet several of their former high school classmates for a reunion of sorts. It was the first time that Kubicek had been asked to drive the two classmates. Accordingly, neither Mike nor Dennis were aware of the terms of Mr. Kubicek's services. So it was a considerable surprise to the two of them when Kubicek told the boys, when he dropped them at their destination at the corner of Peel and Sherbrooke, that they owed him $40, a charge that outraged both Mike and Dennis. After refusing to pay Mr. Kubicek his $40, Mike said that they were prepared to pay $15 at the most, an offer that prompted Kubicek to start yelling in a foreign language, likely Czech or Polish. They both immediately disembarked from the Vauxhall and headed down Peel Street at a brisk pace. They were laughing as they escaped. Kubicek drove down Peel up as far as Ste Catherine's Street. The two boys then headed west on Ste Catherine, a one way street going east, preventing Kubicek from chasing the boys in his Vauxhall. Kubicek stopped at the traffic light at the corner of Peel and Ste Catherine, got out of the car and yelled several threatening epithets at the boys, who couldn't possibly hear them given the distance. Although they couldn't make the exact nature of Kubicek's threats, they sounded frightening enough. Both of them hoped that Kubicek, who had quite a reputation as a drinker, would have forgotten about the incident before all three of them returned to work after the weekend.

As it turned out, Kubicek the cabbie did not soon forget the incident. After work on Monday, he was waiting for Mike and Dennis in the parking lot behind the plant. Mike and Dennis were in the habit of crossing the lot to walk home. Kubicek was leaning on the hood of his Vauxhall when the boys approached him. Kubicek yelled at the two of them, "You two owe me money, $40 you owe me." Mike and Dennis looked at each other with dumbfounded expressions on their faces. "When you going to pay me? You owe me $40.", his voice rising. In fact, he was shouting. People leaving work for their cars paused as they passed Kubicek yelling at the two boys. Mike then asked Dennis. "How much money do you have on you?" Dennis went through his pockets and came up with $8 which he then handed to Mike who was holding a $10 bill. He then faced Kubicek. "Look, Mr. Kubicek, we have only $18. That should be enough for you. I mean, your $40 charge to me is like stealing. I think a cab ride downtown could be maybe $15 tops." Kubicek took a couple of steps toward the boys and his shouting grew louder. "You call me a thief! You two are nothing more than liars. You agree, I drive, and you don't pay. And now, you offer me less than half what you owe." Dennis then made a smart remark, suggesting that he and Mike could do the math too. Kubicek then made a threat. "I go to Morrisette in Personnel about this thing. Maybe he do something." Mike stared at Kubicek and replied with a threat of his own."I don't think Ferry allows its employees to operate taxis around the plant. You could get in trouble." Kubicek stood mute and motionless. Mike and Dennis started to continue home across the parking lot. Kubicek gave the both of both a menacing look. From that look, Mike and Dennis realized that the matter wasn't closed. He put the $18 back in his pocket for now.

⟶◇⟵

Looking for his third summer position at Ferry Industries in the next April, he submitted his application to a personnel officer named Dentoni, who had replaced Mr.

Morrisette, the previous personnel officer. He told Mike that Morrisette had left for another company several months ago. He had been a clerk in the personnel office. Mike said he recognized Dentoni from the previous summer. Within two weeks, Mike received a telephone call in which Dentoni said that he would start a summer position on the second Monday in May. He asked and was told that he would be reporting to Mr. Lecours, the supervisor in the paint shop. He was relieved to learn that he would be no longer be working for Charlie Balfour, plant carpenter. While he was unfamiliar with the new assignment, the annealing and painting of ducts for telephone wires at least sounded better than hanging around with Charlie. In addition, he was informed that he would be getting a raise to a $2.10 an hour, an increase of 25 cents from last year's hourly wage. He was content enough until he was informed that his friend Pete managed to secure a summer job in the Chrysler warehouse on the other side of the Trans- Canada. Pete was getting paid more than twice what Mike was being paid for a much more difficult job. Mike wondered how Pete got the job. Maybe it was his uncle. He sold used cars out of his gas station.

<hr>

He reported to Mr. Lecours for work on the second Monday in May. He was sharing the annealing and painting with a man named Raymond Juneau, a veteran employee who had worked in practically every division of Ferry except for the tool shop and complained about every one of them. It took Mike and his new partner fifteen minutes or so to learn the details of the annealing and painting job which included what to do if either of them fell into the paint trough. Lecours informed the two of them that falling into paint can result in more than messed up clothing, serious injury possible, particularly if any of the paint was either swallowed or got into a person's eyes. It was a two man job, one hanging the unpainted ducts at one end of a conveyor belt and the other unloading and stacking the painted ducts after they went through the paint trough. The colour of the painted ducts was a predictable industrial gray.

Occasionally, a duct would become untangled from the conveyor belt and fall into the paint. Since Raymond had seniority, a status that several of Mike's fellow summer students questioned, Mike was responsible for fishing the fallen duct out of the paint. Every time it happened, not that it happened frequently, Raymond and whoever happened to be in the vicinity would laugh and sometimes circulate the story of the incident to the blue collars in the plant cafeteria where any paint mishap would provide a generous amount of entertainment to whoever was around. Although Raymond took care to ensure that Mike did not injure himself, occasionally he did although not seriously. It was a Thursday afternoon when Mike lost his balance and fell headfirst into the paint. Unlike his other stumbles, this time Mike's head actually ended up being submerged under the surface of the paint. It took him a week to remove all the paint from his face. Fortunately he had closed his eyes. His mother wasn't happy. In addition, he ended up with paint in his hair, which forced Mike to have his hair cut as short as possible, an eventuality that resulted in him becoming a considerable target for merriment around the plant.

As a result of his mishap, Mike was moved to another position in the plant, that of drill press operator where he found himself working for a supervisor named Moe Bouchard, a short, balding man who was gruff and known for yelling and throwing things at anyone who made an error, the most likely blunder a broken step drill, a frequent result of a faulty drill press. Anytime that happened, Moe would yell "machine casse", throw something, almost always a tool of some sort, at the operator clumsy enough to break another drill. The first time Mike broke a step drill, he was told to visit the supply shop run by Leo Gagnon, who had the habit of pretending to ask anyone requesting supplies for a gratuity, after which he would laugh. He would invariably complain about the request, offer up an unusual expletive, withdraw his complaint, and disappear into the bowels of the supply room to look for whatever was being requested. When Mike arrived to ask for a replacement step drill, Gagnon frowned and expressed his usual complaint, "Not another step drill!". Mike offered Gagnon the damaged drill through the cage door of the supply room. As he waited for Gagnon to return from his search for a new step drill, he was reminded of the last time he stood before a supply room door. He was in grade five and he was asking a seventh grader for a Hilroy exercise book. He was in a daze of contemplation when a man joined him in line waiting for Mr. Gagnon. Mike turned to give the man a casual nod. The man grinned and observed. "Let me guess. A step drill, right?"

Towards the end of that summer, he happened to befriend a Ferry colleague named Steve Drury, a full time employee who worked on the assembly line. Drury was a man in his thirties who was rumoured to have spent some time in jail, supposedly for drug dealing, a charge that made him popular among summer students looking for quality weed, a product that they thought Drury could always lay his hands on. He reminded Mike of Roger, who he first met at the Beaconsfield Golf Course when the latter was the head caddie and the former was a rookie. Mike worked with Roger at the Lawrence Plastics Company. Like Roger, Drury was commonly regarded as a working class hero type. So Mike was more than excited when Drury invited him to his place on the shore of Lake Saint-Louis for a swim and a little weed. Drury also said that he wanted to show Mike his cottage out by the lake, a strange objective although Mike never really thought about it. In any event, it was a Friday after work when Mike and Drury drove out to the latter's cottage in the latter's car, a nearly new Ford Mustang, which made Mike wonder how a man on the line at Ferry could afford it.

Drury lived in a small cottage no more than twenty feet from the shore of Lake Saint- Louis. When the two of two drove up to the cottage, there was an attractive woman maybe in her mid-thirties waiting in the doorway. She was wearing a bathing suit, a bikini that barely covered her. She was smoking a cigarette. Drury introduced Mike to the woman. Her name was Allison and she said that she used to live in the Ville-Marie neighbourhood of Montreal. She also said that she worked in a strip club in the Dorval Airport, not a surprising occupation. She also confided that she was divorced, an unnecessary admission that again did not come as any surprise. The three of them eventually shared some weed and a few drinks, after which Drury offered Allison sexually to Mike. It was a promised experience beyond all expectation, sex with a stripper, an adventure that anyone with his limited history with women would not normally forget. But he was reluctant about the offer, almost frightened by the prospect of demonstrating his innocence, if not his virginity, fumbling with the woman who probably began having sex before Mike was born. So he declined, prompting Drury to express a certain incredulity. Allison thought it was cute.

Mike spent the rest of the evening totally wrecked, the weed must have been particularly potent. He had also consumed a few glasses of scotchs. By the time Mike arrived home, Drury had to help him enter his house by the backdoor ---- Mike slept in the basement. The next day, Mike's mother had to enter his basement bedroom to wake him up, it being early afternoon by the time he was conscious enough to barely remember what had transpired the previous evening. On the Monday, he didn't see Drury until that afternoon, at which point he offered him a smirk and a nod as they passed each other outside the locker rooms. The other drill press operator, a fellow summer student named Ron, asked about his evening with Steve Drury. Mike had told him about the invitation for Friday, something that impressed the hell out of Ron. After all, the man was an outlaw. He, like most of the younger employees in the plant, was in virtual admiration of Drury for the same reasons that Mike was. Mike told Ron that the two of them did a little weed and a lot of booze, not mentioning the involvement of his girlfriend Allison in the evening's entertainment.

DON'T BREAK ANYTHING
WEEKS IN THE KITCHEN

The following September, he spent a month bussing tables in a restaurant which had opened recently in a block south of the Trans Canada highway. The place was more like a diner than a restaurant although the owner of the place, a former chef named Mallette, was hoping to attract a better class of patrons than diners in the suburbs were usually accustomed to. He had renovated a former gas station, hired a couple of cooks from a restaurant in the Fairview Shopping Centre and several waitresses from the same place. Mike spent less than a month picking up dirty dishes before the restaurant went out of business.

Mr. Mallette had advised Mike just not to break anything. He didn't.

THE EARLY YEARS
WORK ETHIC TRAINING V

◆━━━━◆━━━━◆

It was rumored that Ferry Industries would not be hiring anybody for the next summer. It was maybe sometime in February of the next year that Mike had run into a fellow student named Ken Turner, who had worked for Ferry Industries the previous two summers and therefore was in a position Mike thought to know something about the employment prospects for the next summer. In any event, Ken told him that Ferry wasn't going to hire students for the coming summer, necessitating the both of them to make other arrangements for employment. Ken volunteered that one of his uncles could probably help him secure a summer position with the Bell Telephone. He also advised Mike to start looking for an alternative to Ferry, that is if he was planning to attend university for another year. Mike was surprised that Ken, with whom he was not particularly close, would be familiar with his plans for the next academic year. After all, Mike was close to graduating from college. However, he had applied to Carleton University in Ottawa to study for a graduate degree in journalism. He never could explain his reason, even to himself, for applying for another year of university, this time in Ottawa, aside from his opinion that his linguistic abilities, or lack thereof, would limit his prospects for future employment in Montreal. It was the second week in February. He had maybe ten weeks until the school was over.

Like he did several years previously, he started canvassing the local area. He had had some success there. Lawrence Plastics was located near the airport while Ferry Industries was above the Trans-Canada in Pointe Claire. In addition, Mike applied to a number of the stores in both the West Island Mall, including the Steinberg's grocery, and the Fairview Shopping Centre. He even cycled out to the airport where he asked about a summer position in a couple of stores in the Dorval airport, including the Duty-Free Shop.

Mike must have applied for maybe fourty or fifty positions over the next eight weeks or so. Whatever case of the nerves he had experienced when he applied for a position varied depending on the reactions of the company representatives whom he approached. Most of the people with whom he met were understandably officious, presumably hoping that they could dispense with Mike as quickly as possible. Mike thought that many of the employees of the companies who may have accepted his applications for employment were tired of receiving them, tired of reading them, tired of selecting a few of them for their superiors to analyze, their selection criteria unknown and then tired of filing them, usually in the company wastebaskets. It was no surprise then that a majority of the officers dealing with any inquiry for employment greeted him with little more than serious apathy. Fortunately, a majority of the staff members who greeted Mike were women who, although usually annoyed with most job applicants, at least provided them with some sort of distraction. On the other hand, some firms, which were usually smaller factories, seldom had a separate individual whose responsibility was to greet visitors. Instead, in such cases, job applicants were greeted by foremen or other employees who would dispense with job applications as little more than simple nuisances. So for Mike and other job applicants, the possibility of successfully landing a summer job was unlikely. So he was getting desperate, so desperate that he had gone back to Mr. Delorme at Steinberg's once in February and twice in March.

It was getting close to the middle of April. He figured that he had few prospects. His nerves, which were usually kept fairly secure, started to fray. Both his mother and his father, not to mention some of his friends, began to ask him practically everyday about his job search, questioning that prompted his anxiety level to increase. While he was normally kind of nervous when approaching potential employers, standard behavior during the years he was looking for employment, he began to have all sorts of difficulty anytime he applied for any job. To compensate for potential attacks of nerves, which were becoming more frequent, Mike sometimes began to fortify himself with a drink from his parents' liquor cabinet, every now and then having to buy a bottle of rye or scotch to ensure that his father didn't notice.

As the end of the school year approached and the need for a summer job intensified, Mike's search for a summer job, any summer job, intensified as well. He enlarged the area in which he began to look for summer employment, investing three or four days a week submitting applications to stores downtown. He thought that his experience as a men's wear salesman in a downtown department store would recommend him although he would take care not to reveal the specific history of the position, specifically the circumstances of his termination from that job, hoping that no one checked. He went up and down Ste Catherine's Street, asking for job applications from practically every retail store from Guy to University, on both sides of the street except for the women's stores which he thought would not consider hiring a male university student for the summer. While he managed to submit applications at most of the stores he entered, he only was able to speak to anyone about a job in only one of every four stores he filed applications. Consequently, he was hardly able to have many expectations about an interview from any of the stores he sought a job, let alone an offer of an actual summer job. Mike had concluded that his journey up and down Ste Catherine was therefore a waste of time. Time was running out.

One of Mike's friends, a guy who named Brian had a summer job at the Dorval Airport. He told him that he had heard that the airport's Duty-Free shop was looking for a retail clerk for the summer season, their previous choice for the job having decided to take another job in the third week of April. He advised Mike to apply as quickly as he could, recommending that he talk to a salesman named Ray Kelly, who was also the assistant manager of the shop. As soon as Mike arrived home after meeting and talking with Brian, he telephoned the shop and spoke to Ray Kelly. He explained the purpose of his call and was pleased when assistant manager Kelly asked if he wanted to apply for the job, a question prompted by Mike's fabrication regarding a retail sales job for the Simpson's Department Store.

Understandably, Mike immediately reacted positively. Mr. Kelly then told Mike to report to him the next day for an interview with the manager, a Mr. Lalonde and himself. He also said that if he and Mr. Lalonde were pleased with the interview, he would have to complete an application form.

They also agreed on 9 o'clock in the morning for the interview. As usual, he would ride his bicycle over. After dinner, during which his parents were pleased to hear about the interview, he called his friend Brian to thank him for the tip.

Surprisingly he guessed, Mike started his position as a salesman at the Duty-Free Shop in the Dorval Airport on the second Monday in May, barely two weeks after he spoke to Mr. Lalonde and Ray Kelly. His mother, who often was dismissive of his wardrobe, particularly since he hadn't worn a sports jacket and tie since he was in high school, had purchased a new suit for him at Tip Top Tailors, the initial purpose of which was to outfit him for university graduation. Fortunately, the new suit was also convenient attire for his new position.

The Duty-Free Shop was situated in the concourse of the airport. It was a rectangular structure, not surrounded by walls but by four glass counters, anchored by a small office in the middle of the shop. Each of the four sides of the shop featured different products for sale, all of which were high quality, brand names. On one side, there was men's wear, shirts, ties and accessories like cuff links, tie clips and pocket squares while on the second counter, there was woman's clothing, mainly sweaters, blouses and stockings. The other two counters provided displays for jewelry, watches and perfumes. In addition, the Duty-Free Shop sold liquor and cigarettes, the brands displayed on shelves about the counters. All merchandise was kept either in drawers underneath the glass counters or in the basement lockers. As explained by Ray Kelly, duty-free shops sold goods to travelers who were about to leave the country. The goods, which must be immediately exported, are free of certain duty and taxes normally applied on goods sold in Canada. Mike didn't tell told Kelly that he already knew that.

Mike, who joined the second sales clerk, another summer student named Susan, learned the details of his position in less than ten minutes it seemed. The two sales clerks, which did more demonstrating products than selling them, basically unlocked the counters, lifted from underneath the surface of the counter the items in which customers had expressed an interest, and showed them to the customers. There wasn't so much salesmanship than waiting for the customer to decide whether he or she wanted to make a purchase. If the customer wanted to make a purchase, Mike or Susan would arrange for the details of the sale transaction, ensuring in particular that the customer had a ticket for a flight outside the country and that customers knew the procedure for picking up the merchandise at the gate of the flight.

Aside from the monotony of selling liquor, jewelry, and clothing that neither of them could ever afford, there were two and even three things that made working at the Duty-Free Shop at the Dorval Airport more attractive than one would think. Mike was romantically pursuing Susan which was relatively convenient since the two of them spent three days a week working the same hours behind the counters. He was hopeful, the evidence being the serious flirting between the two of them. Unfortunately for Mike, regardless of his aspirations,the two of them never had a relationship outside of work, the major obstacle being the fact that she had a boyfriend, who sometimes waited for her after work. To Mike, the boyfriend appeared to be much older than Susan, maybe in his late twenties or early thirties, well dressed, presumably a man with a good job. He drove a small British sports car that he would park in front of the exit doors and wait. Mike's infatuation with Susan hardly diminished, however. his flirting with her continuing.

Strangely, Susan didn't seem to mind the continued flirting either. Their flirtations were definitely novel, so different that anyone who saw them together would comment on their behaviour. Both Ray Kelly and Mr. Lalonde, not to mention a guy named Ross who worked as a general assistant for the Duty-Free Shop and four other stores in the airport, had supposedly noticed that Mike and Susan were in the habit of exchanging written notes to each other practically every day. Lalonde, who was responsible for the store's paperwork, would occasionally come across one of their notes, accidentally left in the daily written receipts. They were usually lines from poems, the titles of which were indicated at the bottom of the note. The poets, however, were not identified, left to the recipient to provide in a subsequent note.

Despite his search, Lalonde could not locate any responses to any of the notes, of which he would came across maybe a half dozen. In his investigation of the relationship, which seemed unavoidable given his curiosity, he was unable to witness any incident, from either his own observations or the observations of others, mainly Ray Kelly or general assistant Ross, showing any physical contact between them. Kelly thought that they occasionally spoke to each other softly, almost in confidence, as if they were in some sort of relationship. But on the other hand, Kelly was hardly sanguine about that impression, actually convincing himself that while it would be an attractive thought, there was no simply evidence that Mike and Susan were having some sort of amorous relationship. Nevertheless, their relationship seemed fascinating, even to Mike himself, who seemed to be pursuing an entirely spiritual relationship. As for Susan, Mike had no idea as to what she thought. He also wondered about whether she and her erstwhile boyfriend with the sports car conducted their romance in such an esoteric manner. He wondered if they ever held hands. He knew that he and Susan never had.

The other element of his job at the Duty-Free Shop was the occasional opportunity to serve well known personalities, if not celebrities over the counters. Most of them, if not all of them were professional athletes, given that Montreal had teams in three professional leagues. In addition, aside from the actually meeting such people, which was exciting in and off itself, not to mention the chance to convince famous customers to provide an autograph and then to sell them expensive merchandise. Finally, there was the possibilities that the shop offered for thievery, a situation that was particularly tempting for Mike, whose previous retail experience involved shoplifting, transgressions that he took care to hide from Lalonde. Fortunately, Mike was able to avoid any pilfering despite the potential the place had for such behaviour.

Susan left her position at the Duty-Free Shop in the second week of August. She intended to attend Queen's University in Kingston but wanted to take some time off before the school year started. On her last day, before she left the shop for the last time, Susan asked Mike for a private moment, during which she kissed him in a consciously passionate manner. Mike almost fainted. Mike remembered that kiss for years but strangely, forget her family name.

STRUGGLING WITH INDOLENCE
PRETENDING TO GROW UP

For several years in the early 1970s, after Mike had graduated from university, having acquired a worthless bachelor's degree in Arts, and spending a few months in journalism school of all things, and a familiarity with a variety of street pharmaceuticals, he drifted from dead end job to dead end job, at least they were dead ends to him. Sure, there was an occasional holiday thrown in courtesy of the friendly people down at the Unemployment Insurance Commission (UIC). Back then, it being more than almost fifty years ago now, it was relatively easy to qualify for and receive such benefits, suffering the indignity of actually working for a living for a couple of months the sole requirement. It was a miracle. One could receive a quick couple of hundred dollars every two weeks for doing absolutely nothing, one's only complaint being that depositing the cheque at any bank was usually uncomfortable, the bright green colour and the large size of the cheque itself enough to identify the recipient as a scofflaw, his or her laziness made obvious to disapproving bank tellers. It was like lining up at the bank with obvious pee stains on your pants. To qualify for UIC, one was supposed to be looking for work but few, if any had ever heard of anyone who was a UIC beneficiary having to produce evidence of ever meeting such a requirement. In any event, the ease of meeting such obligations bred a certain level of cynicism in most UIC beneficiaries, that is if they were actually aware of them. Fact was that the requirement was basically ignored.

While he was not exactly certain, having been so informed by older co-workers who bitterly resented the younger generation taking advantage of what they considered to be "welfare", UIC requirements were not always so effortlessly satisfied. In the mid-1960s, during his first summer job, a regrettable four month stint in a plastics factory, he was provided with a small booklet into which he would regularly insert stamps proving that he was employed during each specific week. If one collected stamps for thirty consecutive weeks, they would receive unemployment benefits, the duration of which he never knew. That had changed by the early 1970s when the requirement was reduced to eight weeks, an extraordinary modification in policy and an understandably extremely popular move among the indolent, of which he was occasionally an enthusiastic member. Although he probably never knew it at the time, it was said that the change was prompted by severe unemployment in certain provinces. Not that any of the lazy UIC bastards cared about its origins, regardless of where they lived in the country. They cashed the cheques, no matter what colour they were, how large they were, and no matter how obvious it was that they were not gainfully employed.

Once out of university, an experience that remained

memorable to him for only the next five years or so, he was compelled to retain full time work, hopefully a position with some sort of a future, employment that would last longer than three months and perhaps allow for some sort of upward mobility. Unfortunately, he was under the impression that the late 1960s and early 1970s had provided the economy with a major proportion of the so-called "baby boomer" generation, who had been discharged from colleges and universities in unheard numbers but offered few job opportunities. It was recognized as a sociological phenomenon that prompted the publication of endless magazine or newspaper articles and libraries full of academic studies. He could not quote any specific statistics regarding the job market at that time although most of his fellow graduates, or at least the ones with whom he stayed in touch, did not seem to have much success in landing a job that precipitated anything in the way of a future. He managed the prudent thing. Like some, he attempted to avoid the entire matter. He decided therefore to stay in school as long as he could. He recalled explaining his decision to his friends that staying in school was preferable to pursuing employment, "It beats working" becoming a refrain for him. Some of his old friends understood, others just wanted to grow up to be their fathers.

After a few months or so wasting his time attending journalism school in 1971/72 at Carleton U in Ottawa, admittedly a pointless move so he could postpone the inevitability of having to secure employment in Montreal, a possibility for which he was not linguistically qualified, he found himself washing test tubes four hours a day for a couple of nervous scientist types at the National Research Council. His stint at the NRC, as pleasant as it was compared to most of his previous labours, lasted until April, at which point the school year was almost over and he would have to start paying for his own apartment, the fee for his stay in a student residence having expired. So he leased a dump downtown in an old house that looked like it was haunted. It cost him the princely sum of $85 a month, a living room/bathroom/kitchen bachelor pad not quite large enough for two. The landlord was a young guy who told him that the house, having been divided into six separate rooms, was owned by his grandfather, who apparently had no interest in selling the joint and had consequently asked his grandson to manage the place.

He was also burdened by a girlfriend named Sharon, whom he was fated to support for more than a year and whom he was to marry within several months. He had weeks to secure employment, the grace period that his last pay cheque from the NRC would provide. In addition, the young landlord said that he was willing to extend them for another month before he said he would have to have them evicted, a possibility that understandably concerned them. in addition, UIC was out of the question. The waiting period was too long and the likely stipend too small a sum anyway to support both himself and his intended for any period of time. He needed a pay cheque. Also adding to his financial worries, which were obvious, was the declaration by his fiancee that she intended to take a couple of summer courses at Carleton, meaning that she would not be contributing to household expenses for at least the twelve months or so, her two summer courses as well as her last two semesters at the Carleton journalism school taking up the next year. Fortunately, the frequency of their romantic adventures, which sometimes included outrageous displays of sexual gymnastics, their passion for each other undisturbed it seemed by their worries, the planning for their upcoming nuptials, now scheduled for sometime in September, as well as his suddenly frenzied pursuit of needed employment all distracted him from any reluctance about their marriage, an example of youthful stupidity if there ever was one.

He applied at dozens of places during the first week of May, going from office to office like a man hawking vinyl siding. On the Monday of that second week of unemployment, his desperation so palpable that he had started to develop a case of the nerves, the beginnings of some sort of anxiety disorder that would bedevil him for the rest of his life. It was an irony considering the frequency with which he was to consume street pharmaceuticals before he developed any sort of nerve problem. He avoided, however, seeking chemical relief from the possibility of a case of the nerves, figuring that showing up high to personnel offices would not impress prospective employees. Of course, the evenings were another matter.

It was during that first week of conducting his serious search for work when he ran into Ray Hiller, an older, married guy who he had befriended after they had both made similar cynical remarks during an introductory seminar on political reporting they had endured during their first week of the Carleton University School of Journalism. Hiller reported that he had recently agreed to return to a previous position he had held as a guard in the federal prison in Kingston. Ray, who had at one time high hopes of securing a job as a reporter at the Kingston Whig-Standard, was understandably, if not bitterly disappointed in his fate, repeatedly expressing regret regarding his waste of nine months studying journalism at poor old Carleton U. The fact that few of their thirty odd classmates managed to land any kind of position in journalism, the exceptions being four students who had previous reporting experience, did little to assuage his gloom, a condition he further illustrated by telling Mike that his wife had left him, a turn of events that may not have been such as a misfortune for Ray, if Mike's memory served.

Ray had wanted to continue his litany of complaints in a nearby tavern, the Ritz, a derelict though historically memorable joint on the corner of Bank and Somerset. It was well known fact that it had been originally been built as a hotel late in the nineteenth century, housing various luminaries, including the occasional federal cabinet minister. It now functioned as one of least popular drinking establishments in the city, a once glamorous lounge transformed into one of the city's few authentic dumps, its only denizens serious drunks and assorted vagabonds. He declined, the appointment he had with someone in a government personnel office around the corner from where he had encountered Ray an unfortunate excuse. Besides, he had less than $2.00 on hand. Ray gave him a respectable shrug and headed toward the Ritz on his own. As he watched Ray walk away, he felt a little less dejected than he had been before he came across Ray fifteen minutes before. He had concluded that Ray's circumstances were more dire than his own. No wonder the guy was drinking in the Ritz he thought. It was the last time he ever saw or heard from him again.

He was therefore surprisingly cheerful when he met with Mr. Michel Nadeau, a personnel officer with the local office of the Canadian tax department. He spent maybe twenty minutes with Mr. Nadeau who must have smoked at least four cigarettes during their interview. For some reason, Mr. Nadeau, who spent the whole time speaking through clouds of smoke, seemed to think that their exchange was somehow humorous, frequently punctuating his comments with short bursts of laughter mixed in with cigarette smoke and paroxysms of coughing. He could hardly understand what was so funny about his barely amusing narratives involving the hijinks in the tax department. Nadeau told him a story about a woman named Donna, who actually did work evenings in a local strip club he claimed, as well as several other stories about clerks showing up for work inebriated and the like. By the time he left Mr. Nadeau's cubicle, he was more familiar with office gossip than he was with actual job for which he was applying. Despite all the comic relief emanating from the loquacious Mr. Nadeau, he did take enough time to inform him that while the local tax office wasn't hiring, the main office, the department's headquarters on Heron Road, might be. He left the place wondering how someone like Mr. Nadeau managed to keep his job, whatever it actually was.

After filing an application at the main branch of the Bank of Montreal on Sparks Street, drawing a sour look from a receptionist who took the form, he returned to their newly leased apartment to find his intended sitting in front of a typewriter topless, an impressive sight that immediately prompted a predictable response. Then, during the enjoyment of a post-coital joint, Sharon handed him a couple of pages out of that day's newspaper, specifically the want ads. She pointed out a quarter page notification of employment opportunities at the Royal Canadian Mint on Sussex Drive. Sharon suggested that he head down there the next day, noting with a certain ironic impertinence that there was nothing in the kitchen but a bag of weed, a bottle of scotch and a half case of Labatt Fifty. When he asked about supper, she did say that she had cashed that morning a cheque she had received from her parents, who lived in North Bay and still thought that their brainy daughter was living on her own, a fiction that would survive until their scheduled wedding in the fall. So they went out to dine at a local Chinese joint less than a block away on Somerset.

At dinner, he had chicken balls, fried rice and a chocolate milkshake while she had something more exotic as well as a green tea. While he was complaining about his day looking for work, she offered him another measure of sympathy, which may have explained her topless stunt when he got home. For the hundredth time he thought, he admitted to Sharon that he would have to take a job that wasn't exactly what he was looking for, needing the money the obvious priority. During dinner that evening, Sharon then again raised her suggestion that he consider asking his parents for money, a proposal that he had always opposed. Anyway, his mother, whose name was actually Ethel, was unlikely to be receptive to any request for financial help. In fact, his mother was more likely to admonish him for his lack of ambition, a complaint that he had heard almost constantly since he was old enough to have a paper route. His father, a generally meek man who still worked as a salesman in a department store, never disagreed with Ethel. Besides, he was determined not to annoy his parents until after the wedding, a point he often made with Sharon. She apologized for bringing up his parents and returned to talking about his job search. She advised him to make himself a little more presentable the next time he went out to apply for a job, even a lousy one. She then insisted that the next time would be the next day at the Royal Canadian Mint. She suggested that wearing a clean shirt and tie might be a good idea, claiming that his usual golf shirt and tan chino combo was not particularly presentable. He didn't disagree with her fashion assessment but intended to go along anyway.

So the next morning, it was a Tuesday, despite feeling a little hung over, Mike forced a cup of instant coffee down his gullet, had a couple of smokes, Player's Light being his regular brand, and then put on his only tailored collar shirt, a tie that he had borrowed two years ago from his father, and a pair of gray flannel pants that he hadn't worn since Christmas dinner at the home of Sharon's parents. He then kissed a barely conscious Sharon and was out the door, heading toward the corner of Percy and Somerset streets, his intended purpose to first catch the Number 2 and then the Number 3 downtown to Sussex Drive where he would present himself to the personnel office of the Royal Canadian Mint, as instructed by Sharon the previous evening. He arrived there sometime before eight o'clock. He found himself waiting with maybe a dozen other applicants in what was basically a guard house. It was placed by the fenced entrance to the Mint, presumably to act as a waiting room for people looking for employment or tourists looking to visit the place. The visitors were greeted by two uniformed men who he later was told were called Commissionaires. They wore imitation military uniforms on which both men actually wore medals, which were most likely legitimately earned, both men looking old enough to have served in World War II. To add to the presentation, they both wore mustaches, like waiters in an old fashioned restaurant.

The other guys waiting seemed as nervous as he was, staring at the floor or ceiling or out the window at the Mint building, which looked like it might have been initially designed as a castle as opposed to a plant that manufactured coins. He had wanted a cigarette but one of the Commissionaires had already announced that there was no smoking, a curious order since he was standing in the doorway to the shelter smoking when he gave it. He managed to relieve his stress by reading the newspaper, a copy of the *Montreal Gazette* which he had picked up that morning between buses at a local news stand called Comerford's Smoke Shop. One of the other applicants waiting with him stood behind him also reading his paper. One of his fellow applicants in the room asked whether he could have a cigarette if he stepped out of the guard room. The response was not unexpected, the Commissionaire that originally gave the order shaking his head and taking an exaggerated drag on his own cigarette, his second cigarette since they had all entered the room maybe five minutes ago.

After another several minutes, a rotund middle age man in a terribly unappealing brown suit arrived, stepped into the room with a purposeful stride. He was toting a clipboard. He introduced himself as Deputy Coin and Metal Director Douglas White, informing the dozen men waiting for direction that he would be conducting a short interview with each one of them, noting with a certain annoyed inflection that he had spoken to several dozen applicants the previous two days. He then held up the clipboard he had been holding and began to read off a series of names, taking attendance as it were and informing them to line up as their names were announced. Mike was announced fourth and took his place in line after an older man who looked like he was or was soon to be down on his luck. He nodded to the man, who had the odour of cigarettes, stale beer and all of their byproducts. The older man, who had taken refuge in a cigarette as soon as his name was called as he was outside the guard house, looked ashen, as if he were frightened somehow, not just nervous but actually scared. As soon as Mr. White completed his announcement and all dozen applicants were properly in line, memories of elementary school momentarily invading his thoughts, he went to the head of the line to lead the procession through the front door of the Mint building itself and motioned them in. As Mike passed him, Mr. White knocked the newspaper he had been carrying out of his hand with a stern but curious observation.

"You won't be needing the paper." he advised, as if he had been carrying a firearm. "I'll be expecting your full attention." He immediately recalled the impression he had formed that there was a military dimension to the Mint that would be revealed to him at some point. Sharon might have put that thought in his head for some reason. In any event, Deputy Director White intimidated him with that comment. He was nervous. He had actually considered stepping out of the line and giving the entire plan up. But he didn't and was soon climbing several stone stairs into the entrance of the Mint itself, past a tall wooden entrance with an ominous black doorknocker. Another Commissionaire was holding it open for them. The applicants soon found themselves lined up for a second time before another wooden office door on the second floor. It was Deputy Director White's office. Again, shuffling nervously, they were then asked to take a seat on one of the two walnut coloured benches stationed on both sides of a long corridor in front of White's office, large windows at either end and several hanging lamps illuminating the corridor. The dozen applicants, six on each bench, stared at each other, waiting.

Within a couple of minutes, a prim looking middle age woman wearing a patterned floral dress that fell well below the knee, opened the Deputy Director White's door and directed the first of the applicants into the office. The middle aged woman's name was Frances Fitzgerald and she was one of only four women who worked at the Mint. There was Gracie and Lillian, two old women who ran the canteen, and a woman named Diane Desjardins who worked for the Master of the Mint. Although he never laid eyes on Ms. Desjardins during the more than two years he had eventually worked at the Mint, he understood that she was unusually attractive and was rumoured to be conducting an affair with the Master of the Mint although no one even saw them together.

The first guy sitting on the bench closest to the Director's door, a short guy wearing a blue blazer that was too large, black trousers that looked to be too small, a white shirt that was missing a button and a plain red tie, walked into the Deputy Director's office with an understandable look of trepidation on his face. Maybe five minutes later, he emerged, a relieved smile on his face, holding a folded piece of paper. It was apparent to him that the short guy had been successful in gaining employment with the Mint. Not knowing how many new employees the Mint would be hiring, he began to feel a little anxiety beginning to collect in his colon, not a particularly rare feeling for him. A second man was invited into the office and the four guys on the bench on that side of the corridor moved closer to the large wooden door. He was now two spaces away. That second man, a slim guy dressed in a green work shirt and matching pants, looking like he was already on the job, casually ambled into the office as if he had been there before. Through the open door, he saw White's secretary greet him with a friendly little gesture and the man nodded to her. He was understandably convinced that the man in the green work outfit would be getting a job as well. Damn, Mike thought, two down and not knowing the number of jobs that were left available ---- millwrights, machinists, general labourers, blue collars all, whatever those jobs were --- his case of the nerves was growing. Sharon would be pissed, so there would likely be trouble when he got home unless things started to look up, that is he if has hired.

The man in the work uniform was ushered out of White's office by his secretary in less than five minutes, stopping at the entrance to exchange a few words with the secretary before leaving her boss's office. Both of them smiled as he left the office. Mike's chances continued to evaporate he thought, unless Deputy Director White intended to hire a dozen new workers in god knows what capacities. The next man up, a guy who looked like he could be a student, was reading a textbook and keeping to hiself, ignoring everybody around him. He had noted that the guy had been carrying the book in the guard house and he had been surprised that White had not knocked that book out of his hand, as White had knocked the newspaper out of Mike's hand. Now he was seated by the old man who was next up for an interview. The man still smelled like he had just walked in from a smoke filled tavern, possibly a place called the Dominion, across Sussex Drive from the Mint, strangely hidden up the block from the General Hospital. The old man was invited into Mr. White's office, his fetid presence hanging in the air like a cloud. Now next to meet with Mr. White, Mike was staring at the man sitting across from him, a man who was returning his gaze with one of his own. It was likely that neither of them had a thought in his head. For a moment, possibly out of boredom, if nothing else, he stole a quick look at the guy to his right, a man he had been ignoring up until now. The man continued to disregard him. He was reading a paperback, the title of which Mike could not identify. It was another publication that had not been knocked out of anyone's hand. Maybe the Commissionaire in the guard house only had something against newspapers. Or him.

Suddenly, the door opened and the old man with the tobacco aroma problem almost stumbled out of Mr. White's office, looking somewhat bewildered. Mike arose from the bench and almost ran not only into the old man but Mr. White's secretary as he entered the office as the old man was leaving it. Mr. White, his unappealing brown suit jacket draped over office chair, leaned forward on his elbows and started to scan the piece of paper he was clutching. It was doubtless his employment application. White seemed understandably impatient he thought, having seen dozens of prospective employees since the Mint placed that advertisement in the newspapers the previous week. He did not look up from the paper at first, launching his first question without benefit of eye contact. Actually, it was more a comment than a question, pretty well predictable in any job interview. It was obvious that White was bored and impatient, an unfortunate combination.

"Mr. Michael Butler is it?", Mr. White said, a predictable opening question. "I see that you have worked summer jobs in factories." he observed, still looking down, a finger trailing down the paper as he was examining the application. "A plastics company, a plant that manufactured chain saws and made duct work for heating and cooling services. And then, a duty-free shop. Right?"

Mike nodded almost enthusiastically and added. "And I was working at the National Research Council until last month."

White grunted an acknowledgement. "Sure, I see that. Part time job, right? And what did you do there?"

"I cleaned test tubes and things like that." answered Mike.

White continued his inquiries about Mike's relatively

mundane employment history. "Cleaned test tubes? You mean, like a janitor?"

"Sort of I guess. I collected the glasses they use in the labs, cylinders, beakers, those sorts of things, put them through an autoclave and then returned the clean glasses back to the labs. It was pretty basic."

White nodded again. "Well paid? It was a government job, right." It was now Mike's turn to nod. "The pay was okay."

"Okay?" commented White.

Mike offered a barely noticeable smile and replied. "Well, it was better than it was at my past jobs, a lot better."

"Well, why did you work at any of those places?" observed White.

Mike was suddenly felling more comfortable. "They were summer jobs ---- the best I could do at the time."

"Understandable I guess." said White with a sigh. "Now, why are you applying for this job?" He said it as if you were surrendering to the inevitability of the job interview, a cliched inquiry for the hundredth time it seemed. White often wondered why he had to ask such a question. After all, why would anyone apply for a job he didn't want, except for those lazy bastards who were looking for a job in order to remain qualified for unemployment insurance, which didn't seem to be the case with Mr. Butler. He actually looked sincere, if not desperate.

"Why? Well, I need a job." declared Mike Butler. There was a pause, dead air as the two contemplated their next remarks. Mike then broke the silence with a question. "The positions you're advertising are for basic labourers, right?" He did not include any reference to machinists, millwrights, or any other job categorization, including the term used as a universal affront to the workingman ---- workee, a class that Mike and most of his colleagues in university avoided but ultimately employed, at least temporarily every summer from the age of seventeen. Before that, it was either a pack boy at a grocery store or a caddie at a golf course. It was the usual blue collar characterization.

White leaned back in his chair and then returned, paper down, hands on the desk, and looked straight at him. "Yes, Mr. Butler, we're advertising for basic labourers." He then offered Mike a thin smile and an announcement. "And I'll can tell you that I can offer you a job here. Can you start next Monday, that is if you check out, which looks like it shouldn't be a problem?"

Mike nodded, a surprised look on his face, surprise and relief. "Yes, I can. And thank you."

White got up and offered Mike his hand. "You're welcome. And could you please report to Mr. Bertrand in Personnel. You may as well go see him now. He's on the first floor. He'll get you straightened out." Mike assumed that there would be some forms to complete, some information to provide, some details to iron out. Mike was relieved but disappointed. He was now back working in a damn factory, the place he thought he had been avoiding by attending college.

With that advice, Mike left the office, acknowledging both Mr. White and his secretary Fitzgerald. As soon as he got out of White's office, his pace quickened, heading to Mr. Bertrand's office as instructed. His office was at the south end of the corridor, identified by a small black sign sticking out from the wall beside his office. A guy dressed in an industrial uniform, dark blue in colour, was walking down the corridor from the other direction. As he walked, he had a frightening grimace on his face, alternatively clenching and then spreading his hands out, and murmuring profanities under his breath. Mike continued on to Mr. Bertrand's office, a little alarmed. He was wondering what had just transpired between Mr. Bertrand and the blue uniform. Maybe the guy had just been fired. He stared back at the guy as he disappeared down at the end of the corridor. He then approached Bertrand's door. He knocked and an accented Francophone voice invited him to enter. Surprisingly, Mr. Bertrand looked to be younger than Mike. He offered Mike a smile, offered him his hand, and waved him into a chair across from his desk.

Bertrand sat back down. "Welcome, I'm Pierre Bertrand. I just got the call from Deputy Director White to make sure you can start on Monday." "That's great. Thanks." Mike replied, still smiling.

Bertrand had several forms in front of him. "You know, you must have impressed Mr. White. He asked me to set up you here almost as soon as you left his office."

Mike almost laughed. As grateful as he was with the news of White's quick decision on hiring him, he had to know. "Why so quick? Is that normal?"

Bertrand then offered a quick laugh himself. "Actually, of the dozen staff he wanted hired in the last week, he decided almost immediately to offer four of them jobs, including yourself. Suffice it to say, he makes quick decisions on almost everything, including by the way letting people go."

This time, Mike did laugh and offered an interesting aside. "I think I saw the latest victim of Mr. White's quick decisions on the way in."

Bertrand suddenly took on a look of apprehension. Mike immediately guessed that he had been right and that Bertrand, Deputy Director White and maybe other people who worked at the Mint were frightened by the guy who had just been let go. Bertrand then went on to explain. "His name is Murray Legault and as I think you've already guessed, he wasn't happy about being let go." Mike moved closer to Bertrand's desk and asked why Legault was terminated. Bertrand had already noticed his move forward and was about to continue his explanation of the circumstances of Legault's departure. "First of all, he's been trouble every since he started several months ago but..."

Mike immediately went to help out. "But?"

Bertrand proceeded carefully. "Well, yesterday he assaulted a guy named Grant Schultz in the punch clock line."

"Why would he do that?" Mike was interested. He was glad, however, that Legault wasn't around to hear Bertrand's explanation.

"He was one of those guys who always wanted to punch out first. Unfortunately, Grant Schultz is also a guy who likes to punch out first."

Mike tried a little levity. "So maybe both of them should have been fired." Bertrand responded. "Well, Grant Schultz has been punching out first for maybe 25 years. It is apparently a tradition here."

"And I guess Legault didn't believe in that tradition." Mike concluded.

"I guess not." And they both snickered, lightly, like it was a secret.

The next Monday, Mike reported for his first day at the Royal Canadian Mint. Further to Sharon's suggestion, if not insistence, he was neatly dressed for the second day in a week, in the same shirt and tie combination he sported to his interview that may have helped land him the job in the first place. He again found himself in the Mint guard house under the watchful eye of a Commissionaire, one who he had not seen during his only other visit. As he had the previous week, he was now standing, this time with three other guys, three guys presumably also starting their Mint careers. All four of them stiffly greeted each other. Mike noticed that two of his new colleagues were carrying paper lunch bags while all four of them were carrying new safety shoes, as instructed the previous week by Mr. Bertrand. Sharon had suggested that he prepare his own lunch. Mike demurred, retelling for the thousandth time the story of his childhood dislike of the school lunches prepared by his mother, resistance that he frequently exhibited by throwing her daily offerings into the bushes on his way to school. He ensured Sharon that the Mint had an elementary canteen; burgers, hot dogs, simple sandwiches, soda, coffee, tea and various packaged cakes. During their conversation of last week, Pierre Bertrand had informed him that two older women, their names were Gracie and Lillian, operated the canteen during the day shift while the evening shift serviced itself, foremen and lead hands in charge of the cash and everything left in the canteen from the day shift. The canteen was closed for night shift, staff working midnights usually sending out for pizza or eating their own bag lunches. Mike was reminded again of his mother's luncheon menu of peanut butter and banana, walnut and cheese, egg and onion and fake smoked meat sandwiches.

A man named Bergeron, Claude Bergeron, who introduced himself with the nickname "Moon", a moniker that no one in the plant could ever adequately explain as long as Mike would work there, arrived to escort them into the plant. He was told that some of his older colleagues had started to call him "La Lune" years ago, "Moon" being the appropriate

Anglophone alias. Aside from his curious moniker, Monsieur Bergeron also stood out by wearing a white hardhat, a strange accessory given that the staff were all required to wear yellow hardhats. Of course, there were some employees who seldom wore hardhats. There was a rebellious melting house guy named Rick and an all around douche bag/maintenance man named Gilles, both of whom were rebuked if caught without their hardhats. "Moon" or "La Lune" Bergeron escorted the four new employees into the locker room where he handed each one of them a large sized grey uniform, just like the one Murray Legault was wearing when he passed Mike in the second floor corridor last week. He briefly wondered whether former Mint employee Legault ever declined to wear his hardhat. Bergeron then handed each one of them a yellow hard hat, a pair of safety glasses, another requirement that Rick and Gilles often avoided, an employee punch card and a combination lock, informing them that they were to wear the grey uniform, the hardhat, the safety glasses, and the safety shoes at all times when they were on the plant floor. Bergeron then concluded his demonstration by introducing them to four empty lockers, pointing to the punch clock, which was conveniently stationed just outside the locker room near the staff entrance and advising all of them to report to Mr. Stanley Peacock, the examining room foreman.

On the way over to the examining room to report to Mr. Peacock, all four of them stopped to use their new punch cards. One of the guys, a large guy whose name Mike would eventually find out was Dave Moore, was informing the other three examining room recruits that their future duties were among the most boring and tedious of the many boring, tedious jobs that were available in the Mint. Dave Moore, who said that he had worked in the examining room during the previous summer, adding that his uncle had and still was working in the melting house of the Mint, further explaining that the examining room assignments were, while the easiest, the least attractive of the many unattractive duties available in the plant. Therefore, as he sardonically pointed out, new employees always did a stint in the examining room before he either earned new assignments or went crazy and quit. He quickly added, an aside at which everybody laughed, that practically anyone can work in the examining room, mentioning a guy named Guy who, according to Dave Moore, "..didn't have the sense to pour piss out of a boot." Two of the other new recruits, including Mike, laughed. A a smaller guy, who looked like he was concentrating on the question of whether Dave's estimation of the guy named Guy was humorous, did not laugh. He never seemed to laugh.

The examining room was a relatively quiet section of the Mint. The noise produced by the other areas of the Mint, the melting house, the rolling and cutting room, the annealing room, and, by far the noisiest area, the press room, where blanks were stamped into coins, made the examining room sound like a funeral home. Foreman Peacock, who appeared to be beyond retirement age, was seated at a desk behind a small weigh scale that looked like, at least to Mike, standard equipment for jewelry manufacturing. Standing behind the scale was a stout middle aged man wearing a white lab coat. Mike was soon to learn that the stout middle aged man, whose name was Ralph, was administering a procedure known as "weighing up", a process of determining whether each sack of coins that had just been examined contained the proper number of coins by weighing each sack. Evidently, a specific amount of quarters, dimes, nickels, and pennies all had specific weights, which staff like Ralph stood behind the scale to check. Mike studied him long enough to conclude that he looked bored enough to be on some major tranquilizer which, once he got to know him, may have been a medical fact. The room was dominated by four large elevated conveyor belts at which two employees would sit at each conveyor belt inspecting, or more officially examining, freshly minted coins looking for flaws or at least pretending to look for flaws. If they were found, improperly struck coins the most frequent discovered defect, they were discarded into a tin can, after which they were ultimately thrown into a furnace in the melting house. Nobody knew how accurate the examiners were.

They were then introduced to the examining room. Foreman Peacock got up from his chair, came out from behind the weigh scale table, shook the hands of all four of them, and motioned toward the conveyor belts. He briefly told them that they were scheduled to take up examining room duties that day, replacing four guys who were slated to be transferred elsewhere. The four were trained by spending maybe fifteen minutes listening to and watching the four guys they were replacing. Mike was to replace a guy named Brian who, after briefly explaining a job that he said a kid in grade school could do, advised him to make sure that he didn't drift off when the belt was running. Mike checked the clock on the wall above the weigh scale. It was ten minutes after nine o'clock in the morning on his first day of work at a full time position. Mike climbed up on the elevated platform and started to examine coins. He wondered whether he was starting a career. He was depressed for the rest of the day, visions of Charles Dickens throbbing in his head.

A CAREER
CLERICAL POSITION I

A fter six months at the Mint, during which time he had worked as a labourer in all three shifts in both the examining and the melting house, he transferred to a position in the press room. From there, he almost immediately applied for a clerical position. In applying for the job, he again was to visit Pierre Bertrand in the personnel department which, as he was to later find out, consisted of only him and his superior, an older man named Royal Plante, who was also the plant accountant. Bertrand explained the job application process: the application itself, the collection of references, which was likely limited to checking criminal records, and the competition board, an expanded interview process during which three people, someone from personnel, presumably Bertrand, and two from the plant, probably one or more of the section foremen as well as Bertrand's boss Plante or Deputy Director White, would assess the suitability of the applicants for the job by having the candidates answer a series of supposedly skill testing questions.

Mike recalled that one of his supervisors at the NRC,

a pleasant woman in her early thirties about whom he had managed to construct a fairly healthy fantasy, had told him that the competition interview was a nerve wracking process that had reminded her of the occasion when she had defended her doctoral thesis in university. She also told Mike that her husband, who also worked with her at the NRC, was so unnerved by the process that he almost had to be hospitalized, an unfortunate reaction she suggested to excessive anxiety medication. Amazingly enough, her husband ended up being offered the position for which he had competed, because, as his wife told Mike, no one else applied for the job. Mike asked why, if her husband was going to get the job by acclamation anyway, they had conducted the board. Marilyn, the supervisor, the man's wife, explained it away with a cryptic observation: "It's the government. That's the way they do things. Doesn't make any sense but it's the government."

Mike knew that at least three of his colleagues in the press room had applied for the same position. All three, as well as four other recently hired Mint employees, shared similar circumstances. In the last year or so, most of the recently hired Mint workers, had attended university or college, two even had degrees, including Mike. This was unusual, at least compared to the educational backgrounds of the older workers. At first, the difference created an understandably uncomfortable relationship between them and the veterans, almost all of whom had worked at the Mint for years. The latter group usually arrived right out of high school, and never even contemplated university or college. Almost immediately, the older guys resented the hell out of the recent arrivals, even the recent arrivals who hadn't gone to college ---- there were two or three who had been hired even though they had not gone to college but looked like they had. At first, it seemed a hair thing. The younger guys were in constant conflict with plant Director Bethel, Deputy Director White, some of the foremen, particularly a fat and frightening looking man named Marcel, and most of the older guys. The two senior managers, Bethel and White, the foremen and many of the older workers had either been in the military or wished they had been. Most of them wore their hair in an appropriately abbreviated style while some, like one of the foremen, a guy named Audet, sported buzz cuts, hair so short that they appeared bald. One guy who worked in the examining room, a skinny individual with a degree in history from Carleton, used to say that Audet looked like a long dead German named Rohm. Nobody ever knew to whom he was referring, that is if such a person ever existed at all in the first place. Many of his colleagues thought that the skinny kid from Carleton had spent too much time standing close to the annealing tub.

Mike was one of the least chastised for the length of his hair, it being relatively short and neat compared to some of the others. Nonetheless, Mike's hair had long been the subject of potential dispute at home. His father, concerned he said with the rising costs of a barber, would cut the hair of both his brother and himself with cheap electrical clippers. He explicitly remembered sitting on a wooden box in his father's workshop, having his hair butchered by a man who knew less about hair cutting than he did about Renaissance painting. Not that it mattered that much. In high school, he was subject to the hirsute edicts of the Jesuit priests who taught him, no hair over his ears or touching his shirt collar the standard. Once Mike managed to leave the suburban comforts of home, he grew his hair long although not as long as many of his fellow students, therefore not long enough to trouble the management of the Mint. He resembled one of the Beatles of the mid-1960s, hair long but clean and neat, the kind of observation that parents used when accepting the gradual lengthening of their sons' hair. Compared to some of his fellow students, who maintained hair that looked dirty and disorderly, Mike appeared relatively acceptable to the adult world, a distinction that even his friends like to point out to him, as a reproach. Besides, Sharon liked his hair.

On the other hand, a guy named Gord Flood was undoubtedly one of the main targets of Mint management. Not only was Flood's hair long and unruly but he would respond to warnings about his appearance with flippant, if not sometimes profane comments, often turning comments about him back to the commentators themselves, referring to the appearances of the bosses, mainly their hair and their girth, with usually humorous result. In addition, he almost never wore his hard hat. Although he had been given a hard hat, he had been issued, at his own request, one that was much too small, the result being that when he was told to put his hard hat on, he would attempt to place the hat on his head, prompting his irate superiors to order him to request a hard hat that actually fit, a command that Flood simply ignored. He did carry a pair of safety glasses in the breast pocket of his grey work uniform although the lenses of the glasses had been removed, an irony that usually went unnoticed by his bosses. Inspired by Flood, who oddly enough had become somewhat of a hero to former university/college students who Flood himself thought were lame and fat headed, Mike and some of his co-workers would often go out of their way to make fun of their superiors. They would make smart ass remarks, some better at it than others, offer strange, if not funny gestures, and, especially when tourists were passing on a tour, break into song, popular hits and fake opera the usual choices. No one could remember what prompted the singing but once they started it, they couldn't stop, no matter how often the tour guides --- there were two of them, both summer students ---- admonish them to quit their vocalizing. Apparently, it was disturbing the tourists.

In any event, despite the occasionally unorthodox misbehaviour of these workers, most of the plant foremen, except for the tyrannical Marcel Audet, claimed that he would have fired the lot of them if he had the authority. On the other hand, the boys were thought to be as productive, if not more productive than most of their older co-workers. Plant accountant Plante, who did not often share the views of his fellow managers, thought that the kids as he called them, had a real future with the Mint, a prognostication with which most of the kids, Gord Flood notwithstanding, would have found depressing.

On the other hand, many of Mike's co-workers did not live up to Mr. Plante's high estimation of those he thought had a bright future with the Mint. Like his summer job experiences in other factories, Mike observed that the Mint had a number of workers who demonstrated a predictable level of inertia or more precisely, work avoidance, something that he and others observed in one form or another for the remainder of his career in the government. Mike recalled that there had been a co-worker in every factory he had ever worked who advised him that the most appropriate approach to getting along in any job was to always look busy, particularly if you weren't. In the Mint, there were several classic examples of workers who had adopted this concept. There were a few in each section although the size of the room and nature of the production being pursued limited the number of those who had managed to transform loafing into a job description.

One of the more obvious examples of this practiced

laziness was a relatively young labourer named Dan Gaudreau, who was the one of the plant's janitors, a position that most of his colleagues envied since it involved little more than ensuring the locker rooms and the washrooms were relatively clean. Anyone with any sort of sense could fulfill his duties with minimum effort, without breaking a sweat, the general estimation being that Gaudreau only had to work maybe three hours a day, the remainder of the day he could invest at playing euchre in the canteen or taking a nap in a locker room. His nickname was "Dan the Gojo Man", a reference to the industrial cleaner he used in his job. Aside from their envy, most of his co-workers wondered how he managed to land a job that required so little work. In that regard, unkind things were often said about suspicious relationships he may have had with a number of managers. It helped that Dan Gaudreau was generally ingratiating to almost anyone he came across, especially anyone who was his superior, doing favours for the bosses, delivering pizzas, going to the bank, buying liquor and beer, passing notes to dancers at a local strip club for big Norm in the melting house, that sort of thing. Anyway, he had noted that while the plant had a few lazy bastards drifting through it, Dan Gaudreau was a wonder to management. He was a favourite.

***

Mike was not really surprised when he won the competition, which basically consisted of filling in a one page application and answering a series of ridiculously simple questions about the job, current events, and basic arithmetic. He was informed by letter that he was to start as a CR-3, a clerical position that was to pay him $7,500 a year, a little more than the $3.50 an hour he was making as a basic labourer in the press room, which had still been his position when he got the notice of his promotion. He started the new position on a Monday, having been informed of the new duties on the previous Thursday. He was told by his new boss, the accountant Plante, that he was a so-called officer now, whatever that meant, and that he should dress accordingly, meaning that he would have to resurrect his tailored collar shirt, the tie that he had borrowed from the old man two years ago, and those grey flannel pants he wore to the original interview.

He remember feeling pretty strange that Monday when he walked into the examining room, where he had been assigned to work as a clerk that first day. He was now responsible for ensuring that the coins that had been examined and bagged by foreman Peacock and his crew were properly weighed and placed on pallets for eventual shipment to banks, presumably all over the country. Mike was now behind rather than in front of the small scale that weighed each sack of coins to ensure that it contained the right number of coins. Mike had seen the procedure many times when he had been working in the examining room and had realized that the job hardly posed any effort,. Once a bag was weighed, it was placed on a pallet. Once the pallet was full, that too was weighed but on a much larger industrial scale, it was placed in the plant vault, where it awaited delivery. The weight of each pallet was recorded and summarized at the end of shift so that the production from each specific section, melting house, cutting room, press room could be measured and reconciled. As long as the summaries of each shift's totals were without significant discrepancy, appropriate allowances being made for waste, clerks like Mike would approve the shift's work and the pallets would be secured in the vault.

Mike soon realized that without his approval, examining room staff would have to wait until whatever differences that had been discovered by an officer like Mike would have to be reconciled. He was now a member of management although that status was not generally accepted by the guys on the floor. In fact, some of the boys, particularly a lift truck driver named Ron Lindsay, who used to suggest that Mike was barely out of high school and therefore was hardly qualified for the job. Within months, however, Mike and Lindsay became casual buddies, playing together on the Mint hockey team, a sort of panacea among co- workers. Ron Lindsay eventually became comfortable with a moniker that had been assigned to him ---- "Lindy 500" ----- a reference to both his name and his habit of driving his lift truck at dangerous speeds around the plant. Everybody, including most particularly the older hands, thought Lindsay was the best lift truck driver they had ever encountered.

A CAREER
CLERICAL POSITION II

◈━━━━━◈━━━━━◈

While the clerk job was easy and dull as hell, it did pay Mike an annual salary that he thought sufficient, particularly now that Sharon had graduated from Carleton U and was working in the government, drawing a higher salary than him. It didn't take him long to get used to his new position. He found it absurdly easy, at least compared to his previous lines of work. He was basically keeping the weekly books for his shift, the only complication, which was occasional, being when the books were out of balance, when it appeared that the production from one department did not match the production from the others. One veteran clerk, a middle aged man in a lab coat named Ralph who now shared the same position as Mike, described the accounting process of making sure that what went to work in the morning came back at night, within relatively narrow margins of error. It was basically an empty bureaucratic exercise in simplicity, a job that most of Mike's colleagues said could be done blindfolded, although Mike was not aware of anyone who had ever tried to perform their duties that way.

It came as no surprise then that within a couple of

months of starting the position, Mike was demonstrating the same ennui as the rest of the clerks who held the same job, some of whom sometimes demonstrated a tentative hold on reality. There was a guy named Andy Nolan who had the curious habit of sometimes adding the date, in abbreviated form, to the list of pallet weights that had been recorded during the shift that he worked. This undoubtedly resulted in significant discrepancies in the shift's output, showing differences in weights of thousands of pounds. The first time it happened, the entire shift was held up for at hour until management gave up on the unsolved mystery and sent everyone home. Three days later, someone, it was presumed to have been Mr. Plante, the accountant, noticed that someone had added a number starting with a one and showing no dot between the fourth and fifth digit in the list of pallet weights. Once the suspicious number was found in the ledger for the day shift for November 12, 1972, there being more than a 1,000 pound difference between that number and the other numbers recorded for that and every other day, someone, again presumably Mr. Plante, surmised that whoever had recorded the number had written in the date ----- 121172 ---- rather than the weight for the pallet that was supposed to have been recorded. It was explained that the discovery had been made after someone noticed that both the date at the top of the page and the erroneous number in the list of pallet weights were not only identical but were also written in the same script, the handwriting of Andy Nolan.

Everyone who was informed of the resolution to the mystery of the erroneous weights was suitably entertained and would repeat the telling of the story to anyone who would listen. Finally, anytime there was a discrepancy in the list of pallet weights, Andy Nolan's name would invariably come up, even after Mr. Nolan had left the Mint for a more promising position, a development that seemed difficult to believe in view of his performance on the job at the Mint. Somebody said that the Department of Foreign Affairs had hired Nolan. Most people believed that it could be true although they found it difficult to believe.

Mike had started to hear the stories of theft almost as soon as he started. They were rumours really, usually dispelled as soon as they were told, particularly by the more experienced staff who presumably had heard these stories, or some variant of them, for some time. It was predictable given the products produced by the Mint --- currency. That explained the unusually strong security measures, unusually strong for 1972 that is, that the Mint applied. All staff had to wear a pass on their person to enter the grounds and at all times when they were working. Everyone but management, who were fortunate enough to have a special pass, were not permitted to leave the premises until the buzzer to signify the end of a shift went off. Medical appointments were excepted, but required a note from the doctor. Most of the staff compared the procedures at the Mint to a medium security correctional institution.

Despite the security, stories about the theft of currency were fairly common. Most of Mike's co-workers admitted that the occasional pocket full of purloined dimes and quarters was typical. Most of his co-workers would openly wonder why many of the coins in the canteen appeared to be freshly minted, the source fairly evident. Gracie, Lillian and Mr. Plante, who were all responsible for handling the cash in the canteen, simply ignored the obvious, the amounts involved hardly worth any sort of complaint. Mike never pursued such low grade theft, memories of a number of teenage shoplifting incidents, not to mention his misdeeds at the T. Eaton Co., enough to dissuade him from resuming his career as a thief.

There was also the story of a guy who supposedly lifted a full sack of quarters from the examining room and hid it in his locker. The narrative, which may or may not have been true, then goes on to describe the thief as carrying in his trousers a portion of his take out of the plant on a daily basis. The man, who remained nameless but apparently worked in both the examining and press rooms, went on to regularly transport three or four dollars worth of quarters, anywhere from twelve to sixteen coins every second or third day, skipping a day or two to cover his tracks or so he cleverly thought. Within a month, he had moved maybe $100 out of the stash in his locker. He had calculated that, at that rate, it would take him almost a year before he would need to steal another bag of quarters. The story came to a comic finale, however, when the individual involved decided to modify his technique of stealth so that he could more easily and more profitably transport more coins out of the plant. He apparently started wearing cargo type pants to and from work each day, having concluded that he could more easily escape detection if his trousers were equipped with larger and more pockets.

Once he began wearing the cargo pants, he could, and apparently did sneak up to forty quarters a day out of the place without arousing suspicion. That was $10 each time he wore his new pants out of the plant. At that rate, he could empty his locker of stolen quarters within six months as opposed to a year. In any event, he was wearing his new cargo pants when a Commissionaire who was actually paying attention to the employees filing out on a Thursday afternoon made a complimentary comment on the man's new cargo pants, in which he was carrying at the time forty stolen coins in the six pockets provided by his cargo pants. The man behind him in the line agreed and patted him on the seat of his new pants. The man doing the patting immediately felt some coins in his back pocket and wondered aloud whether the man with the cargo pants intended to use a lot of vending machines in the new future, perhaps at a nearby bar which had video poker games. The Commissionaire was suddenly interested in the man's pants and immediately began to pat the cargo guy down, just like on television. According to witnesses, and no one was quite certain as to the identity or identities of the witnesses, the stories having been conveyed from employee to employee like bad jokes, the cargo guy looked suddenly petrified. People who were there all thought the man actually started to pee his cargo pants. The Commissionaire began to turn the guy's pockets out, having asked for the small garbage pail that was sitting in the guard house. Again, according to witnesses, or whoever was telling the story at a specific time, the quarters he was pulling out of the thief's pockets were hitting the garbage pail like broken glass. Once the Commissionaire was finished with his search and counted the recovered coins, he announced to the assembled that the cargo guy was attempting to remove $9.50 from the Mint without permission.

Surprisingly, the stolen coin perpetrator was simply fired, the possibility of arrest discarded when Mint management concluded that if they were forced to arrest a man who had been quietly walking out the front gate door with stolen coins in his britches, the questions that could be raised might well prove embarrassing to the people who allowed him to steal the coins in the first place. After the man was caught, every clerical officer was interviewed by Mr. Plante and foremen Audet and Peacock, their purpose to determine how the man managed to steal and hide a full bag of quarters. If anything was ascertained, it was never revealed to anyone else. When his locker was opened, they found an open bag of coins. It was weighed and was discovered to contain approximately $800, suggesting that the thief was sneaking coins out in his trousers for at least a couple of months. Since he did not have any close friends in the Mint, having worked in the place for less than six months, no one really knew where he went after he was terminated. One of the press room guys claimed that he saw him about three months after the incident, working in a downtown office building. The general scuttlebutt was that the guy managed to land a better position although how nobody knew.

Maybe eighteen months into his career in the Mint, another worker, this guy's name was Carpentier, was caught throwing two bags of quarters over the back fence on the midnight shift. He was caught because the first of the two bags managed to land on the hood of a police cruiser which just happened to be driving by on Saint Patrick Street, a street which curved behind the rear of the Mint about thirty feet below it. Carpentier had climbed the iron fence behind the Mint, lugged the two bags, one by one, up to the top of the fence and then threw each over. One hit the police car while the other landed ten feet from their intended target, a parked pick up truck. The police in the car on which the first bag of quarters fell stopped and then watched as the second bag landed in the bed of the truck. They immediately detained the driver of the truck, a woman who also happened to be married to Mr. Carpentier who was caught less than twenty minutes later. Everyone who heard about the attempted robbery was quite entertained. It even made the newspapers.

A couple of months later, during which time Mike did not become aware of any further transgressions by any of his colleagues, he was assigned to the midnight shift, an appointment that brought him under the supervision of a man named Art Trudel, who was the most senior officer on the premises and therefore was in charge of the shift. Trudel was a middle age man who drove a nice car, seemed to smoke a lot, and had worked the midnight shift for years, or so he claimed. On Mike's first midnight, Trudel walked into the clerk's office, a relatively small space enveloped by plywood walls, containing a desk, two chairs, a filing cabinet that may never have been opened, and a cot that was reserved for Trudel. After a couple of minutes of exchanging pedestrian pleasantries with Mike, Trudel laid down on the cot and told Mike not to bother him until the shift ended in the morning unless the building was on fire. He then closed the door, which was then locked behind him. Mike was immediately told that Trudel usually spent his shift sleeping, the explanation being that he had a day job, whereabouts unknown, and needed the rest. Sometimes, though, he would report at the start of the shift at 11:30 pm, hit the showers in the locker room, where he was the only member of the clerical staff to maintain his own locker, change his clothes and spend some time in a nightclub across the river, returning to get some sack time and changing clothes again before his shift ended at 7:30 am. Trudel apparently worked an average of five minutes a shift, not bad Mike observed, for the $12,000 he made annually. When Mike had the temerity to ask why no one had ever said anything to any of the higher ups about Trudel's unorthodox working habits, he was told him that no one ever crossed Art Trudel, adding, in a presumably facetious aside, that even the Master of the Mint Stewart wouldn't consider moving on the guy. No one seemed to know on what basis Trudel was protected.

Mike liked the midnight shift, not everything about it but enough. It was quieter, only the press and examination rooms were working. Mike would only have to do any actual work every hour or so when the examining room would present sacks of coins to be weighted. For the rest of the shift, he would be in the basement playing table tennis, a recreation at which he would come to develop a considerable expertise. Either that, or composing what he thought were entertaining notes to his buddies on other shifts or Sharon. On that point, he was beginning to worry about his relationship with Sharon. Since he started at the Mint, almost six months back, the differences in their interests and points of view was getting wider and more obvious. After all, she had secured a good job and was now associating with people who didn't have much in common with the working class heroes at the Mint. Mike continued to grow alienated from Sharon and pretty well everyone else with whom he had forged a relationship in school. Fact was he was self-conscious about, if not embarrassed with the job, a lowly clerk in the Mint, hardly the occupation to which he had aspired while he or any of his fellow students were still in school. He avoided any of his former classmates when he happened to come across them in the real world, particularly if they ended up with jobs in journalism. He understood that three of his former classmates had found positions with the offices of government ministers, two with Toronto advertising companies and at least half a dozen others found positions as television or newspaper reporters. He was jealous, envious, and almost ashamed. Sharon said that he shouldn't care but he began to suspect that she really didn't mean it.

As time went on, it was predictable that Mike would move closer to the guys at work rather than his former classmates, not to mention Sharon's classmates. Aside from the unavoidable socializing during work hours, Mike started to spend a lot of time drinking with the boys at work, an activity with which Sharon had little if any interest, further causing more problems at home. He joined the Mint hockey team, which provided Mike with another excuse to pursue socializing with the boys at work. He started to regularly patronize a strip club called Rick's. By then, he had become close friends with a fellow clerk named Jeff Peters with whom he shared a shift every three weeks or so. Aside from playing on the hockey team together, they bonded during a shift in the melting house, where they weighed out the ingredients for what everybody called pots, a concoction that was melted into a slab of copper that is eventually rolled, cut, and pressed into pennies. Working in the melting house, it had become easy for the two of them to get close since they had little to do but engage in conversation. Like Mike, Jeff was another university graduate who now found himself in a purgatory of drudgery, all that academic endeavour now rendered forgettable. In the melting house, there were only two clerks and a lift truck driver to prepare the damn pots. The two clerks usually had plenty of time to converse, the task of measuring out the ingredients for the pots almost as mind numbing as weighing the bags of coins in the examining room.

Mike had known Jeff by reputation, a reputation as a presumably moody individual who didn't talk much, was sometimes abrasive, effected a thousand yard stare that frightened some people and looked like he might have lifted weights. He had played junior and later semi-professional hockey, a talent he would soon demonstrate as a star on the Mint hockey team. During their early conversations in the melting house, athletics was the chief issue, a topic which they both discussed with some enthusiasm. Although Jeff, based on his hockey career alone, could be said to be an accomplished athlete, it was an assertion that seemed to embarrass him somehow. Even when discussing sports that first week in the melting house, he did not raise his hockey exploits, or at least the specifics of his hockey exploits, until Mike asked him if he had played, which paradoxically led to a lengthy account of Mike's own hockey career, which basically ended on the third line of a high school team that lost more games than it won. Jeff continued their conversation by casually mentioning his own hockey career, which culminated with two years on a Montreal junior team. Mike was familiar with the team, having played with two guys on that high school team who unsuccessfully tried out for the junior team on which Jeff had played. When asked, Jeff confirmed that one of his past teammates had actually made it to the pros. Mike was quite impressed, not only by the fact that Jeff actually played with someone who had achieved this but that he hadn't boasted about it. In that regard, Mike knew a guy in university who used to constantly mention that he had played on the high school football team with a guy who ran track for Ohio State University. Jeff was definitely not like that. He may have been the diametrically opposite, quite reticent about discussing any of his hockey endeavours. Aside from sports, remarkably enough, they discussed their shared interest in poetry, a pursuit which would have gotten big laughs had it been spread around the plant, particularly if it were applied to Jeff, who had a reputation as a moody tough guy, hardly the pedigree of a poet.

The two of them started to hang out together, not only at work and on the hockey team, which Mike had to convince Jeff to join, but after hours from work, a habit that began to bother Sharon who thought Jeff a little rough for her taste. When they were not on the same shift, which was fairly often, they would leave notes for each other in the clerk's office, confirming the general opinion that while they were both "generally okay", their presence on the Mint hockey evidence enough, they still acted weird sometimes. They also encouraged each other in the art of smart aleck comments and actions. In addition, early in their relationship, they attracted the unusually close notice of management when they prepared so many melting house pots that they were ordered to stop working and take a couple of paid days off.

They also pulled some memorable pranks and instituted several strange pastimes among their colleagues during their eighteen months or so working together at the Mint. In celebration of the bizarre bureaucracy they sometimes had to endure, they would sometimes accurately record the pallet weights of the sacks of coins they were checking for their shift in Roman numerals rather than numbers, that was when either of them happened to be in charge of the accounting for the examining room. When the clerks for the next shift went to balance the accounts, they would note the substitute Roman numerals, prompting frustration and confusion. Most of the time, unless the clerk or clerks on duty during a subsequent shift could actually decipher and then transform back to basic numbers, the Roman numerals were included in the daily balances, to be then incorporated in the weekly reports to be completed by accountant Royal

Plante. Although he did not find the boys' pranks with the Roman numerals humorous, he was envious, recalling, however briefly, a couple of incidents involving his own youthful tomfoolery, one involving grocery deliveries and the other when he and several of his pals were breaking into houses to which he had been delivering newspapers.

The boys only used the Roman numeral gimmick three times before Plante called the two of them into his office. Plante was on fairly good terms with the boys as he called them, particularly with Mike with whom he sometimes played table tennis. "I'll talk to them." he told his seniors, all of whom wanted to suspend them, if not fire them. The majority of his superiors knew and disliked Mike and Jeff, thinking that both had bad attitudes although they usually agreed with Plante that that was never reflected in their work, a judgment that still annoyed them. They were both called into Plante's office on a Tuesday afternoon to face the music. They were working the melting house that day and did not have any warning as to their meeting with Plante. They were on pleasant terms with Plante and, although they figured he would have to bring up the Roman numeral nonsense, they thought, as they discussed on their way up to his office, that whatever rebuke they were about to receive would be relatively minor.

They were right. Plante was alone in the office when they arrived, personnel guy Bertrand presumed to have been asked to excuse himself. Door open, he was sitting behind his desk, didn't get up when they came in. There was only one chair positioned in front of the desk. Jeff looked like he was about to take the chair but Plante waved both of them away. As the three of them expected, Royal Plante spoke first, with a peculiar little smirk on his face. "So what in holy hell were you two guys doing with those damn Roman numerals in the ledger? Some people don't know Roman numerals you know. I do but some people don't know ---- it caused some problems for the guys who didn't. I had to listen to them complain. I had to check some of those ledgers himself, you know, to make sure they were correct."

Both Mike and Jeff were looking down. Jeff was the first to look up. He looked straight at Plante, matching his smirk with one of this own, and spread his arms out like he was about to tell a joke. "It was just something to do, you know, to break up the boredom. We didn't mean anything." He then looked at Mike, who nodded and added a confirmation. "Jeff's right. We really didn't mean anything by it. It was just, as Jeff says, something to do. Just a stunt."

Plante almost laughed and exclaimed. "A stunt? Just something to do!"

Jeff just nodded, still offering Plante a smirk, while Mike seemed somewhat abashed. "I know it was stupid, but we were bored and we thought...." said Jeff.

"And you thought it would be funny, right?" Plante was finishing the thought. "Like you guys are always fooling around like that."

Mike offered some further elaboration. "But it was a little entertaining, you have to admit." Jeff looked a little surprised. He knew that his comment would not go over well with Plante who, predictably, did not agree. Plante was not definitely not entertained. "You call confusing the hell out of some of the guys downstairs and annoying the rest of them entertaining. It was not that entertaining."

Both Mike and Jeff sheepishly shrugged and waited for Plante to continue his observations. He did. He had managed a small arc of a smile, almost involuntarily.

"Look, I know you two like to play pranks and all." Mike and Jeff both knew it was a reference to the melting house pots incidents, it having been Plante who had to ask them to stop working, their efforts to overload the melting house and the adjoining rooms with pots a memorable prank. There was a silence for a moment, a moment during which Mike noticed that Royal Plante had a copy of Penthouse magazine on his desk, a corner of the magazine sticking out from under several daily reports. He wondered if Plante noticed.

Plante seemed lost for a moment. Moments went by. He then threw up his arms, hands went to the desk to push himself to his feet, and exhaled deeply. "Look, boys, just don't do anything like that again, please." Plante then swept the two of them out of the room. Both of the forgiven miscreants were almost out the door when Plante called after him with a surprising admonition. "Don't forget, you two have a game tomorrow night. Big Norm would be pissed if you guys didn't make it." Big Norm was Norm Leduc, the coach of the Mint hockey team.

A PROMOTION
CLERICAL POSITION
INTERRUPTED

S ix months later, Jeff had left the Mint, having accepted an offer to play for a professional hockey team in Holland, following a recommendation from a former teammate named Boyd who had played junior with Jeff five years previously. Aside from Mike, no one with whom he had worked seemed to regret his early retirement. Two weeks later, Mike was coincidentally promoted to a sort of shift supervising job, a head clerical position that entailed ensuring that the work of an individual shift was correctly completed. Everyone thought that it was related to Jeff's departure, thinking that maybe Mike could now straighten himself out with no smart aleck nonsense, no sarcastic remarks to management. Plante thought that he could transform Mike into a career man, maybe his own replacement in twenty years or so, an ambition he sometimes used to mention to Deputy Director White who thought the idea ludicrous, calling both Mike and Jeff disrespectful punks, a characterization he usually applied to anyone under a certain age. A man embittered by unknown forces or unknown events, White sometimes wanted to fire everyone working at the Mint, his secretary reporting that she would sometimes hear him yelling into the telephone about the stupidity of someone or another. She would also hear him discussing this someone or that someone with Plante, who would then found himself defending this someone or that someone. Mike and Jeff were among the most popular someones. So when Mr. White was told that Plante had offered Mike a promotion, he was not happy although he did not ask Plante to rescind the appointment, a power that he seldom exercised no matter how little he thought of the individual Plante promoted. It would, however, be an acting appointment, until such time as a proper competition board could be established.

He didn't even mention the promotion to Sharon who, having graduated several months back from Carleton University, had landed a position providing information services for the Department of Agriculture. He was still embarrassed and, aside from regular sex, both of them probably wondered why they were still married although the question likely occurred to Sharon more often than to Mike, a development that eventually led to Sharon finally ending things four years later, by which time the Mint had become a memory.

Mike lasted another eighteen months at the Mint, mainly on the midnight shift. He would spent most of that shift playing ping pong in the basement against all comers, claiming the unofficial table tennis championship of the Mint for the duration of his term there. It took Sharon less than a year to move to a better job at the Department of Fisheries & Oceans. While their relationship hardly improved, the fact that at least Mike's friend Jeff wasn't around didn't make it any worse. Tired of hearing about the monotony of his Mint job in particular, that is when he actually said anything about his job at all, any stories about the characters who worked at the Mint having little entertainment value to Sharon, she offered to support him for an unspecified period of time if he resigned from the Mint. It did not make much of an impression on Mike who thought she had been kidding at the time she said it. The two of them eventually established a regular rhythm to their lives together. Except for sex, which was average most of the time but occasionally spectacular, they would avoid being personal with each other, behaviour that sometimes seemed peculiar but actually reminded both of them of their parents.They didn't spend that much time with each other, Sharon often asking Mike to leave their apartment on those evenings when she was hosting a dinner or a cocktail party for her colleagues from work, none of whom he had ever met. Mike thought that she was possibly having an affair with one of them, a situation which didn't seem to bother him. In fact, the idea appealed to him for some reason. To be honest, Mike often wondered when she was going to ask him to move into the one of the other two bedrooms in their three bedroom luxury penthouse apartment.

Mike and Jeff had become pen pals during his sojourn in Holland, the kind of relationship that he had not pursued since he was seventeen, at which time he was exchanging missives with a girl he had met during a summer vacation in New Jersey. Anyway, he and Jeff's correspondence was similar to the exchanges they used to conduct when they were on different shifts at the Mint. Both of them had literary pretensions, notions that they demonstrated almost exclusively between each other, submitting poems and short stories to each other rather than to potential publishers, their confidence hardly meriting such ambition. Mike found Jeff's letters particularly good diversions, amusements that he not only eagerly anticipated but would sometimes reread several times, the adventures about which Jeff wrote in his letters were well worth the wait pretty well every time. Whether the stories Jeff related were fictional or not were irrelevant, the comparative excitement of Jeff's life in Holland made Mike feel like he was living a profoundly bland life. Jeff would personify that characterization by opening each of his letters with the salutation "Dear Clerk" which conveyed the message that Jeff was having a helluva time in Holland, it was practically a permanent vacation, while Mike was not. After all, Jeff was getting paid, not much Mike understood but enough to get by, to play hockey while Mike was getting paid to add up numbers and record them in ledgers, five shifts a week.

It was on a Tuesday afternoon when Mike announced his intention to leave the Mint. That morning, Deputy Director White, an antagonist it seemed from the day he started, was standing in the examining room wearing his customary shit brown suit. He was talking to "La Lune" Bergeron, his dumb white hardhat in his right hand. As Mike was walking by the two of them, heading for the clerk's office, White turned away from Bergeron to Mike and called out. White was staring at him, apparently examining him, leaning closer, his hand on his arm.

"Mr. Butler, looks like you need a haircut." White commented, a surprising comment since Mike's hair was relatively short, at least to him. It was an unexpected comment since Mike couldn't remember the last time White had bothered anyone about their hair, the entire issue now seemingly overlooked by a man whose preoccupation with his subordinates' hair having been influenced by current fashion, even the Prime Minister now had long hair. He had appeared again to have reversed his position on hair. So he repeated his observation. "Yes, I think you definitely need a haircut and soon." He offered him another reflection, an accusation in fact. "And I saw you in the melting house last week without your hardhat."

The latter comment amused Mike, seemingly a joke to him. He seldom wore a hardhat in the melting house or anywhere else. He was a supervisor, a head clerk. He thought the position had given him an exemption from the hard hat rule. He wasn't sure, however, about whether his position provided him with any sort of immunity with nonsense like hard hats. He simply didn't know. He provided Mr. White with a timid smile, no intention of being clever, only to pacify White a bit. He was joking, wasn't he?

"You're kidding, sir, aren't you?" asked Mike, the arc of his timid smile curving down. The expression on White's face was stable, no change at all. Bergeron started to walk away, a little wave of hand in departure. "La Lune" obviously wasn't interested in participating in any potential dispute. White responded, surprisingly. "Mr. Butler, I want your hair cut by the end of week." He didn't say anything about the hardhat. "And if you don't, I'll have to suspend you until you get it cut." White then stood back and followed Bergeron out of the examining room. He never understood the reason for White's sudden command, even when he thought about later.

By the end of that day, Mike had formally ended his term of employment at the Mint. He did not know quite the reason for the timing but obviously his discourse with White that afternoon had prompted him to make a decision that he had on his mind for some time. Plante tried to talk him out of it, telling Mike that he thought he could ascend to his job in a couple of years. He told Sharon about his decision when he returned home that evening. She reacted with predictable resignation, almost shrugging and then asking him if he had any plans for the future, not specifically another job but some sort of plan. He proposed that he return to his first ambition, to become a writer, at least long enough to see if he could actually succeed. He had always fantasized about a writing career but never really took such an aspiration seriously, at least not as seriously as he thought authentic writers would have. Sure, he had written in high school and college; short stories, poetry, the occasional appearance in the college literary magazine the sole objective evidence of a talent that he thought he may have possessed. He was pleased, if not relieved, surprised but understanding, when Sharon said that she did not disagree with the plan, reminding him that she was making enough money for both of them. In other words, he did not need to work, particularly at a job he could not abide.

So he began to write seriously, his only current exercise in the literary arts being the letters he continued to exchange with his friend Jeff, who was still playing hockey in Holland. Jeff was delighted with the news that Mike had left the Mint. For the first couple months of his rejuvenated writing career, he was actually producing stories that seemed, at least in his own mind, worthwhile. Sharon, who aside from Jeff was pretty well his only supporter in his literary endeavours, read the first few short stories with some enthusiasm, assuring her husband that they may be worthy of publication. In addition, his correspondence with Jeff remained optimistic, at least in their own amusing, cynical way. But by the third month of his new career, his enthusiasm for writing started to wane. He couldn't explain it, even to himself, even to Jeff who had suggested that his pen pal had contracted a condition he called "mechanics depressive", a fictional psychiatric term that Jeff had invented after misreading a similar word in a magazine. Mike had been working for weeks on a story about a high school janitor struggling with a crisis of faith. He just couldn't seem to settle on the story line although he was pleased with the creation of the main character.

In addition to a significant case of what he thought was writer's block was an inability to come up with an appropriate name for his main character. He usually used names of people from his past, his elementary and high school school classmates a particularly rich trove of character names. But for some reason, Mike just could not decide on a name for the high school janitor. He had selected at least two names of students who he remembered from his grade seven class: Greg Fenwick and Jack McPhee. He only remembered them because they flunked a lot. But he couldn't decide between either of them and went back to attempting to break his writer's block. It was convenient therefore when he ran into a guy named Ed around the same time. Mike worked with Ed in the press room at the Mint and played a couple of games with him on the Mint hockey team, that is before Big Norm cut him. Ed, who was a strange individual with a number of equally strange friends, was surreptitiously known as the plant's pharmacist, a source for every kind of legal and illegal drug imaginable, or at least imaginable by a relative innocent like Mike.

THE BANK
CLERICAL POSITION REBORN

◆━━━━━◆━━━━━◆

It was maybe six or seven months later. Since he had left his job at the Mint, Mike had started to write a book, an ambition he had long contemplated but never actually pursued. Over the last few weeks of unemployment, Sharon had grown displeased with Mike's inertia. Although she said she still supported his literary career, however untested it may have been, it was obvious that her patience was growing thin. She started asking him for an oral report on his daily literary output, sometimes even reading the pages he had produced that day. Fortunately, once she seemed to have reached her limit of tolerance, Mike already had completed eight short stories. Sharon encouraged him to locate a list of book publishers. Sharon had surprisingly suggested that he look for companies who might consider actually publishing his stories, as extraordinary as he thought that might be. Aside from the publication of several literary works in college, including a visual poem written in the shape of a bird which was a prize winning entry in a college newspaper contest, as well as several short stories that, while not awarded any prizes, were regarded highly by several of his classmates, not to mention an instructor named Corrigan who taught an introductory course in creative writing.

In any event, as fanciful as the idea seemed, Mike had initially decided to investigate book publishers in both Canada and the United States. He had discussed his plan with former college associates, including someone named Coleman who apparently had been published himself, several short stories that appeared in U.S. Magazines. Coleman, however, advised Mike to consider literary agents rather than publishers, most of whom were located in New York city. While Coleman had managed to attract an agent named Grant Balfour, he made a number of suggestions, giving Mike a list of recommendations. However, a practical obstacle presented itself. Unlike the circumstances confronting Coleman, Mike was compelled to consider submitting the stories themselves rather than simply attaching a summary of the stories to a letter to prospective agents, Coleman's advantage being the fact that one of Coleman's uncles was in fact a professor of literature at Columbia University in New York City. It was understandable therefore that as his nephew, Coleman would benefit from his uncle's recommendation for retaining a local literary agent. Consequently, he was able to attract an agent named Daniel Chambers who managed to ensure that a number of his short stories appeared in U.S. literary magazines, including a few publications with which Mike was familiar. In addition, Coleman had told him that a fairly prominent U.S. publisher was seriously considering a collection of Coleman's short stories in book form.

Unfortunately, while his classmate Coleman was to provide Mike with advice on possible publication of his stories, he could not or perhaps would not offer him any assistance, including approaching the literary agent representing Coleman. In other words, Mike would have to pursue a literary agent and the potential publication of his short stories on his own. In consultation with Coleman and his wife Sharon, Mike developed a list of ten literary agents located in New York and composed a letter that would be attached to the short stories that he proposed be published. However, Mike faced a major obstacle. He had typed the stories on an ancient Underwood, purchased by his mother when he was in college. There were eight stories, almost 200 pages and he had to arrange for copies to be submitted to potential literary agents. He soon determined that if he submitted his stories to ten individuals on his list, it was likely that it would cost him a considerable amount to copy and mail them. Since he was not particularly prosperous, his UIC stipend was a little more than three hundred dollars a month, he didn't think that he could cover an estimated $150 to copy and mail the stories. He asked Sharon for financial assistance. She agreed to help him out but warned that her contribution was somehow contingent on Mike's efforts being successful.

It had to be almost two months, during which time he started to apply for jobs, further to Sharon's firm suggestions, which were repeated almost daily. He had finally begun to receive letters from some of the New York literary agents who he contacted. Fact was Mike had received replies from three agents, namely Thomas Dentonti, Lester Fagan, and William Stanford. Letters from all three thanked Mike for his letter and his collection, which was received, but only one expressed any real interest in representing his collection of short stories.

His name was William Stanford and he wrote a three

page letter to Mike in which he evaluated each of the eight short stories which he had submitted to him. He praised all eight of the stories and suggested that he would probably would not have difficulty in getting the stories published either individually, in literary magazines, or as a collection. In either event, the letter informed him that Mr. Stanford he would need $400 from him to research the market and proceed with contacting potential publishers. While Mike was quite pleased with the offer in Mr. Stanford's letter, he could not meet the financial requirements. While he initially thought of approaching Sharon for the $400, he decided that he would try to convince Mr. Stanford to provide him with some sort of installment plan, telling him that his financial situation was "abysmal", a characterization that was only partially accurate in view of Sharon's offer of financial assistance. So he wrote Mr. Stanford another letter, thanking him for his offer, pleading poverty and asking him for a financial accommodation. He was relatively optimistic about a favorable response from Mr. Stanford. He had nothing to do but wait. In the meantime, he had started on another series of stories. He had decided to base the future collection on incidents from his past.

He had to bide his time for almost three weeks when he received a package, not a letter but a package. It was obvious that Stanford was returning his manuscript, which demonstrated that Stanford was not interested in acting as his literary agent book, not if his client was destitute. In his cover letter, Stanford wrote that he declined to act as his agent because such a client would become dangerously dependent on his agent, looking for a quick sale at a unreasonably low price. Stanford indicated that such clients often are hard to deal with, usually making their transactions unsatisfactory.

He ended the letter by wishing him well and expressing the hope that he could find a publisher for his collection.

With his hope for publication of his collection of eight short stores having disappeared, at least at the present time, Sharon escalated her pressure on Mike to go back to work. While she hadn't changed her financial offer to him, still willing she said to support him, she said that his continued indolence was not good for his future, recommending that he start applying for a career and not just a way of making a living. She didn't mention his pursuit of writing, realizing that he was fortunate not to have confided his failure to attract a publisher or an agent to her. News of that lack of success would obviously increase Sharon's pressure on him and strain the hell out of his relationship with her. In other words, it could put their marriage in jeopardy. He started to invest a lot of time studying the business section of the Globe and Mail as well as the classified advertisements of the local papers. He was no longer writing, at least not every day which had been his habit, his previous project of basing his stories on his own history on hold for now. So he started to make lists of positions for which he could apply, limiting his applications to posted professions that seemed to have a future. He went through a few previously unappealing opportunities, like insurance, government clerical posts, and automotive sales. He came across a notice in the Globe and Mail regarding openings in the Bank of Montreal trainee program. He later found out that Sharon had come across the same notification a couple days after he did but realized that he already knew about it.

In addition to the Bank of Montreal, Mike had plans

to submit applications to a dozen companies, including four government departments as well as the Public Service Commission itself, three retail stores, two advertising companies, both of which were located in Toronto, and the Bank of Montreal. Aside from a covering letter in which Mike mentioned any notice that may have been published in any newspaper, Mike included a curriculum vita that he had composed with Sharon's assistance, a document with which he had been unfamiliar. Sharon seemed relieved when she found out about his efforts to secure a decent position, an opinion that she demonstrated later with an evening of spectacular coitus. Within a couple of weeks, he had received the first reply to the twelve missives he had sent to prospective employers. It was predictably curt, an obvious form letter from a personnel officer in the Department of Industry, Trade and Commerce. There were two paragraphs that read like they came out of a vending machine. When he showed it to Sharon, she laughed and said that he should not have been surprised with the robotic tone of the letter. It was, however, surprising to Mike since he had never applied for a job by letter, perfunctory application forms or interview his only experience. Mike did not keep the letter.

Over the next week or so, he received similar letters from two other government departments as well as the Public Service Commission, the latter recommending that he take the government clerical examination, a formal testing for individuals desperate enough to want a job as a government clerk. He also received a letter inviting him to come in for an interview with a couple of Bank of Montreal officials at the Ottawa headquarters of the bank. The letter informed him that the bank was considering him for its management trainee program. Although the idea was foreign to Mike, applying to a bank being a suggestion by

Sharon who said that banks and the government usually provided solid career paths, which sounded to Mike like it was a threat. When he shared the letter with Sharon, not only was she pleased but she immediately urged him to accept the bank's invitation. Again, they had surprisingly intense sex that evening, making Mike consider that maybe their sex life was contingent on his career prospects, an idea that he usually rejected as old fashioned and profoundly chauvinistic. If he had ever expressed anything along those lines to Sharon, she would have been justified in hitting him with one of those heavy glass ashtrays. Or so he believed.

So he accepted by telephoning the main office of the Bank of Montreal to arrange an interview. He managed to schedule one for the next Monday at 10 o'clock in the morning. He started to develop a case of the nerves almost immediately after he put down the telephone. To Mike, it was like making an appointment with a malevolent dentist. He usually didn't react that way but he seldom faced a situation that could precipitate anxiety of any kind. While he had applied for a number of jobs, and in fact had been successful in obtaining a number, his previous experiences with job searches having involved cursory quizzes between employers who were only interested in hiring people for the most basic of jobs. But he was now under the impression that his upcoming interview with the two Bank of Montreal officers would be far most serious than he had previously experienced. Sharon sensed his growing agitation and offered to practice with him. She said that it would be important for Mike to perform adequately if he hoped to be offered a trainee job with the Bank of Montreal.

He and Sharon participated in three so-called mock interviews before he was relatively ready for the interview. There was no doubt that he was nervous about the appointment, having had little sleep the night before, so much so that he had gone into the living room to watch television, the only available programs old movies and minor celebrities demonstrating worthless products for people who were dumb enough to want more of them. In the morning, after bidding goodbye to Sharon who wished him good luck by cheerfully slapping his backside, he actually considered fortifying himself with a couple of large glasses of cheap scotch, an antidote anytime he felt nervous about anything. He resisted.

He arrived at the Bank of Montreal headquarters on Sparks Street a little more than fifteen minutes before the scheduled ten o'clock appointment time. For some strange reason, a reason that he could never quite fathom even when he thought about it later, he felt like he was checking into a hotel. He was standing there without any luggage, he wasn't even carrying a briefcase, an accessory that he never thought was required but later learned probably was. There was a receptionist at the top of the marble stairs that greeted visitors at the building, an Edwardian structure that was built before World War I and was commonly regarded as having no architectural equal in Ottawa but to the Parliament buildings. Suitably for the surroundings, the receptionist was a middle age woman who was sitting before a large walnut colour vintage desk with a black and gold name plate identifying her as Miss Eleanor Stubbe. She was wearing a pair of ornate spectacles on a jeweled chain around her neck. Mike strode up to the desk and stood before Miss Stubbe. Not surprisingly, he was a trifle intimidated.

He stood before Miss Stubbe, waiting for her to notice him, a delay that consumed a couple of minutes. He was a little weak in the knees, almost trembling. His stomach was turning, his bowels close to erupting. Finally and fortunately, she spoke. It was now ten o'clock, the scheduled time for his interview. She looked up and pointed to a wooden bench against the wall to her left. "Please have a seat. Mr. Parks will be with you in a few minutes." Her voice reminded Mike of his second grade teacher, Miss McCarthy, who looked like the Wicked Witch of the West and sounded as frightening. He took a seat on the wooden bench, feeling like someone awaiting sentencing, and stared into the cavernous environs of the Ottawa headquarters of the Bank of Montreal. The place looked like a cathedral but without pews, trays of church candles, statues, frescoes of the signs of the cross, pulpits, and most importantly, altars. There were batteries of tellers on both sides of the bank, between which were ornate tables upon which customers filled in forms to deposit and withdraw funds from their accounts which, due to its location, were probably more fulsome than those in other bank branches. Mike had another, maybe his final observation. He had the impression that practically all the bank's customers seemed better attired than most although he noticed that there were elderly clientele who were not as well dressed as most of their fellow patrons.

As he was gazing about the bank, a young guy carrying an expensive briefcase emerged from a doorway just to Mike's left. The young guy was in a hurry, looking somewhat disappointed. Mike was not disappointed, only nervous. He had less than a minute or so to scrutinize who he had concluded was one of the other competitors for the trainee position when Miss Stubbe called out to him. "Mr. Butler, Mr. Parks is ready for you now. His office is through that doorway to your left." Mike went though the door and headed to the office, the door to which was a quarter open. Mike approached the door and gently knocked. Mike inched into Mr. Parks' office and heard his voice, firm and unequivocal.

"Mr. Butler, come on in. I'm James Park. I'm the assistant director of the personnel department in Toronto and head of the training program for the bank. I'll be interviewing you for the position you've applied for." Mr. Parks was a tall, courtly looking gentleman who was dressed in a gray houndstooth suit with a maroon tie and matching pocket square. He looked as noble as Miss Stubb looked frightening. He then invited Mike to sit down in one of the two chairs in front of his desk. He sat down, hoping that his anxiety had stabilized. He was hoping to keep his bowels from embarrassing him.

Parks began the interview with an obvious question. He felt like he was in the principal's office. He felt he was wearing a t-shirt and a pair of sweatpants.

"Tell me Mr. Butler, why did you apply for this position?"

"Well, I need a job and my wife thought that a position like the bank is offering might provide me with, you know, a future." Mike responded just as he had planned. He had actually practiced. He wanted to sound honest, which he was.

"Are you sure that you want to work in banking?" Mr. Parks asked casually, as if he was offering a cup of coffee. "You don't sound too convinced. Besides, what made you decide on banking?" He hadn't really anticipated that Mr. Parks would be asking him that question although he should have guessed. He answered the only way he could. And it had the added advantage of being the truth. "No particular reason. I tried a couple of banks, an insurance company, a department store, and the government. My wife and I, mainly my wife thought that if I was looking for a career, and she kind of told me that at my age, I should definitely be looking for a career and places like banks offer such an opportunity."

Mr. Parks offered Mike a broad smile and looked like he was on the edge of laughter. "Well, I would have to admit that you seem to be honest, maybe more honest than most of the applicants I interview." Mike moved forward in his chair and seemed to be more interested then he previously had been. Mr. Parks then turned to discussing Mike's employment history, which seemed understandable since this was, after all, a job interview. "I see that you don't have that much experience with office work. I see that you had a part time job working in a department store, a summer job working in the duty free shop in the Montreal airport and your last job, responsible for a shift in the Mint. The work there, as far as I understand it, corresponds in a way with working in a bank but I think therefore you are still qualified. Don't forget that this is a trainee position. So we're not looking for anybody with any actual banking experience."

Mike was almost pleasantly surprised. It sounded like Mr. Parks might be reckless enough to actually hire him.

It was twelve days later when Mike Butler received a letter signed by Pierre Nadeau, Director of the Training Department of the Bank of Montreal in Toronto. The letter informed him that he had been accepted for the bank's training program to be held over the first four days in

October in the Hilton Garden Inn near the Toronto Airport. The program was to start with a welcoming reception party on a Monday evening followed by the three days of training. He felt like he had just won a raffle, feeling like he was going to summer camp. For her part, Sharon was so ecstatic with the news that she, aside from standard spectacular sex, offered to take him shopping for new clothes, his business wardrobe still limited to one jacket, three dress shirts, two pairs of dress pants, and four ties that he had borrowed a long time ago from his father. He alternated the outfits between night shifts at work at the Mint. Mike pointed out to Sharon, who often commented on Mike's lack of variety in work clothes, that a Mint clerk named Pelletier wore the same ensemble under a grimy white lab coat every single shift. None of Pelletier's colleagues seemed to notice his lack of variety in work apparel. None of Pelletier's colleagues would have cared either.

He was looking forward to shopping for new duds, not having purchased anything new aside from new underwear since before he met Sharon. On the other hand, however, he was generally worried about two things, actually attending the training program itself and flying for the first time in his life. Further, he was worried that several years of college and a number of low level jobs could be regarded as a management position could qualify him for the job. He was nervous about being nervous.

⸻⸻◆⸻◆⸻⸻

He managed to survive the airplane ride to Toronto without breaking into the airport lavatory in a panic. Nonetheless, both stewardesses were eyeing him suspiciously throughout the flight, particularly since he had ordered and was denied a third double vodka on a fourty minute flight. He stumbled climbing down the stairs from the airplane and almost fell down on the tarmac, suggesting that Mike might have had that third double vodka before rather than during the flight. He was the last passenger to retrieve his suitcase, which was carrying a new suit, two new shirts, two pairs of new casual slacks, a new cotton sweater, and a new pair of shoes, all of which had been purchased by Sharon. In addition, his case contained underwear, socks and a binder full of material provided by the bank. He later thought that he should have included a bottle of vodka and maybe some weed. At least, he didn't lose his bag. Waiting for a taxi out by the airport exit, he noticed that there were two or three other recently disembarked passengers who could be attending the bank training session. In fact, his cab driver remarked that he drove five other passengers to the Hilton Garden Inn near the airport earlier in the day. It was three o'clock in the afternoon. Mike checked in and was assigned room 703. The welcoming reception was scheduled in an hour, time for a shower and a change of clothes. After that, all applicants were invited to dinner.

⸻

After a shower, a change of clothes into business casual and a beer from the mini-bar, Mike went down to the reception where he was faced with maybe twenty people milling around. The anxiety started warehousing in his stomach like a virus. He stood there nervously, feeling like he was wearing clown bloomers. waiting to be welcomed, until a tall, middle aged looking man with a sparse mustache, the obvious host for the evening, walked up to Mike with his hand out. He introduced himself as Stanley Fleury although it was unnecessary since there was a prominent name badge affixed to his chest. Before Mike had an opportunity to identify himself, Mr. Fleury handed him a badge although it did not include a name, only a Bank of Montreal insignia and the location of their eventual branch. Mike then introduced himself, at which point Mr. Fleury acknowledged him as a resident of Ottawa and asked him if he was happy with the accommodations, noting that the bank had been using the Hilton Garden Inn for its training sessions for Ontario since it opened five years ago. He then escorted Mike into the reception room, where there were maybe ten people waiting to begin their careers with the Bank of Montreal. Mike was approached by a waiter who asked for his drink order. Mike asked for a beer and followed Mr. Fleury around the room where he was introduced to the trainees who had already arrived. Fleury then said that six more people were expected.

The occasion reminded Mike of the freshmen orientation gatherings he had attended almost ten years ago although most of guests back then were barely out of high school. He remembered, a memory that he wanted to share with guests who he thought might have similar reminiscences. It was a key feature of what the school called "frosh week", a festivity that was intended to welcome the first year students to the university. To many first year students, it was their first experience with serious drinking. Further, almost half of the celebrants were females, which was remarkable since most of the boys, Mike included, never came across many girls who drank alcohol it seemed until they attended freshmen gatherings. It didn't seem to make much of a difference to the social success that either the boys or girls had with the opposite sex although there were exceptions. A year before he entered university and therefore had an opportunity to attend "frosh week" activities, Mike had met a girl at a CYO dance who was drunk enough to laugh at everything he said. A month later, the girl become his date to his high school graduation dance, an event that disastrously concluded when she passed out in the washroom of a Dunkin' Donut out by the Dorval Airport outside Montreal at seven o'clock on a June morning.

Within twenty minutes or so, Mr. Fleury announced that the full group of trainees group was in attendance, eighteen in all, and invited them to take a seat in a large room in the adjoining dining room. Eight of the diners were women. Mike was seated between a woman named Kate from Toronto and a guy named Jimmy who was was scheduled to do his training at a branch in Kingston. Kate looked to be in her early twenties, just out of college, not university. She had an endearing smile, appealing enough to appear in a Bank of Montreal commercial, a fetching bank teller attractive enough to make the banking a pleasant experience. Mike was immediately smitten, at first sight it seemed, until she spoke, asking where he lived. She sounded like she was attempting a Bugs Bunny impersonation, her voice reminding him of someone who was joking. Kingston's Jimmy, who had been casually eavesdropping on their conversation, tried to join it by attempting a rather shaky version of Yosemite Sam. He then laughed. Neither Kate nor Mike laughed. Jimmy quietly apologized.

Mr. Fleury, understandably seated at the head of the table, stood up and began to introduce the trainees individually, ten men and eight women, eight from the Toronto, five men and three woman, four from Ottawa, equally divided between men and women, and three people each from Hamilton and Kingston. He learned that Kate's full name was Kate Leahey, good to know if he wanted to be familiar with her room number although he also thought the idea a little inappropriate. Mike did not recognize the man or the two women from Ottawa, which for some strange reason he thought disappointing. Aside from the introductions, Mr. Fleury provided the group with a mercifully brief pep talk in which he commended the group on successfully gaining entry into the bank's management program. Although all of them were generally paying attention, except for maybe Jimmy of Kingston, who didn't seem to listening to Fleury's spiel as opposed to staring at Kate, and a guy from Toronto who looked like he was asleep. Fleury didn't seem to take note of either of the trainees who weren't paying attention to him. By the way the three waiters arrived to serve them more drinks and distribute the Caesar Salads. Jimmy ordered another double.

Both Jimmy and Mike spent dinner, there being a choice between chicken, fish and pasta, attempting to engage Kate in conversation. Since Mike was seated to Kate's left, he had an obvious advantage in any conversation competition, Jimmy tried to overcome it by approaching the man to Kate's right with a proposal to switch seats. That man's name was Frank but he seemed to be more interested in talking to his other seatmate, a man named Walter, and therefore declined what must have seemed to be a curious invitation, a game of musical chairs, so to speak. In any event, Jimmy was forced to lean across Mike to talk to Kate. Not only did Kate find Jimmy's physical machinations irritating, she also found his attempts at chatter annoying and ultimately unsuccessful. It didn't really matter that Mike was generally bashful, at least at first. Despite her timid appearance, Kate was talkative, a practice that must have really annoyed Jimmy who had spent at least twenty minutes trying to interest her in any sort of discussion. Kate and Mike invested most of the dinner and a drink after dinner in the bar of the hotel talking about themselves. Mike started to think that the two of them were a couple. He did, however, have to tell Kate that he was married. Kate was not.

Mike remembered the training sessions almost perfectly. They were held in a room with four rows of small tables and chairs, trainees separated by the locations of their branches, which began the next morning with a pudgy guy named Art Cantwell, wearing a three piece suit and red braces, standing before a large blackboard. For reasons most of the class could not fathom, he spent more than two hours outlining both the history of the bank and its current corporate structure. It was like listening to a seminar on "Beowolf" in which an elderly professor spoke old English. Mike was reminded of high school when he took ancient Greek and almost all of the students compelled to take the class stayed awake by punching or pinching each other every time the teacher had his back turned. After Mr. Cantwell had completed his presentation, Jimmy, who had managed to develop a reputation as a sort of unofficial class clown the previous evening, suggested that if one was still sane after paying any attention during Cantwell's symposium, one should consider applying for a job in insurance sales. While the comment drew a few laughs, Mr. Cantwell, who happened to overhear Jimmy's observation, was mildly offended but never responded. Mr. Fleury, who was sitting in the back of the room, did not appear to be paying attention to Cantwell, having heard his spiel dozens of times, mercifully announced a thirty minute coffee break.

Mike, who had spent last night's dinner sitting by Kate

Leahey, mumbling through his attempts at conversation, nervously resumed his pursuit of her and nudging his way beside her while waiting for a cup of coffee. She was standing away from him. She was pouring herself a cup of coffee. Mike greeted Kate quietly. She answered with a charming little smile and turned toward him. She said that she had some trouble staying awake but suggested that at least that was more than she could say about some of their colleagues. She also mentioned that at least Mike's friend Jimmy was listening, at least some of the time. Mike nodded and explained that Jimmy wasn't exactly his friend. Kate had motioned toward Jimmy who had been talking to three other people, two guys from Toronto and a woman she thought was from Hamilton. The three of them had obviously been listening to Jimmy. She had concluded that Jimmy seemed like the kind of guy who always needed an audience. She also said that she wondered why Jimmy was training to be a bank manager.

The next two sessions, before and after lunch concerned the minutiae of everyday banking. It was helpful. Mike's experience with banks was limited to maintaining a bank account, starting in the second grade at St. Louis elementary school. Every week, every Monday, he would deposit a quarter into a savings account, filling in a deposit form. Every Friday, he would receive an updated savings book. By the time he finished the second grade, he had a savings book that showed he had $9.48 in his account, including $.23 in interest, not that he knew what bank interest was. In fact, he had to ask his mother what interest was when he asked her to keep his savings book for him.

The afternoon of the first day through to the second morning, all the trainees started to role play as bank tellers, taking deposits, providing cash to other trainees role playing as customers seeking withdrawals and other banking requirements. Many sought advice on other matters that may have had something to do with everyday banking: inquiries on loans, mortgages, safety deposit boxes, and minor matters like travelers' cheques, money orders, certified cheques, cashier's cheques, money orders and stuff like that. Basically, Mike and the rest of the trainees basically learned how to provide some services and how to direct customers to colleagues who did. Finally, further to questions from more than a few of the trainees, the instructors told the pupils that customers would raise issues that ranged from advice on their wills to what they should wear to a wedding.

In addition, an official from the bank's personnel department gave them guidance on methods of how to deal with complaints, The official, whose name was George McMahon, explained that most of the objections directed at bank tellers or any other bank employee concerned domestic disputes between husbands and wives, the concept of joint accounts and even separate accounts for husbands and wives being most pervasive. In response, McMahon suggested that anyone making such complaints would be appeased if sympathy were expressed and the complaint never judged as anything other than legitimate. Mike whispered to Kate, who happened to be sitting beside him, that McMahon seemed to be talking about marriage counseling rather than the complaints from bank customers.

McMahon ended his lecture by pointing out that, aside from issues related, directly or indirectly, to banking, customers complained about the languages spoken in the bank, the weather, the political situation, the length of the skirts of the younger girls waiting in line, the selection and volume of muzak playing in the branch, and most significantly, the length of the lines waiting for service. It was in this context, that Mr. McMahon told the group that customer protestations concerning delays in service from the tellers, particularly on paydays, were doubtless the most frequent and the most aggressive. One trainee from the Toronto delegation interrupted, telling the group that some days, Friday lunches in particular, tellers were standing at all six wickets waiting for abuse, the lines of annoyed customers snaked out the bank and around the corners of adjacent streets. In addition, for further entertainment, the trainee from Toronto, whose name was Bruce McGarr, also informed the group that there was a restaurant around the corner which often provided bank customers with take-out while they were waiting. In response, the manager of McGarr's branch had installed two garbage receptacles standing by the entrance every Friday, the branch manager having established a rule that no one could enjoy lunch while in the bank. One of the tellers, an older woman named Marilyn was opposed to the edict for no other reason than she reportedly didn't like the manager.

That evening, during the farewell dinner, at which a Bank of Montreal Vice President Campbell gave a short valedictory, Mike's nascent relationship with fellow trainee Kate took a decidedly fortunate turn, or so he thought. Again, he managed to secure a seat at the dinner table beside Kate, during which the two of them appeared to be a couple, or so many of the other trainees thought. In fact, several trainees, not to mention Mr. Fleury, were convinced that Mike and Kate occasionally held hands, a gesture that prompted those who noticed it to exchanged bemused glances. On the recommendation of Mr. Fleury, Mike was selected to read the Bank's Mission Statement at the close of the meal. Mike's allocation was greeted warmly by the group, including Kate who kissed his cheek and whispered something in his ear. He contemplated that something for several months after the training session was completed and the trainees had returned to their branches to apply whatever it was that they had learned during those two days.

"It's too bad you're married and it's too bad you live in Ottawa.", she had said.

He had been working in the branch at the corner of Laurier and O'Connor in Ottawa for a couple of months and he was still fantasizing about Kate Leahey and their conversations during the training session, most particularly her last words to him. He actually thought of calling her at her branch in Toronto a number of times but resisted the urge until he began to forget about their romance, if that is what it was. He then had begun to worry about accidentally referring to Kate anytime he and Sharon spoke or interacted in any way, including most particularly in the bedroom. Over the next couple of months, however, his efforts to have Kate fade from his thoughts began to succeed, his daydreams about Kate were gradually replaced with daydreams about at least one of the tellers in the branch. On the other hand, it wasn't long before he and Sharon began to drift and, though he had forgotten for the most part about Kate, his obsession with the teller began to affect the deteriorating relationship with Sharon, until unfortunately Sharon, one rare evening after they actually had dinner together, told him, if not ordered him, to pack up his possessions, mainly his clothes and record albums, and move into his own place. She gave him a month and left the room. Mike was stunned.

The next day, however, Sharon withdrew the command, claiming that she had had too much to drink at dinner.

Aside from his romantic fantasies, as pointless as they seemed, Mike's duties at the branch were tedious but varied, which didn't help much but at least gave him time to contemplate the personalities of the other people in the branch, prompting him to start writing again. It was something he hadn't undertaken since his efforts to attract a publisher failed several times and he had started to pursue a more conventional career, like for example working in a bank. However, while he was contemplating composing character profiles of his colleagues at the branch, he also had to perform the tasks that his position in the branch had allocated to him. For the first month, he stood behind a teller's wicket, accepting deposits, providing withdrawals, and dispensing advice on a variety of banking issues that were not handled by the humble bank clerk or teller. He was the only male teller providing service to customers most days, the only other man who ever took a turn at that position being a short, dumpy guy named Fred who filled in on busy days when one of the regular tellers was not available. Mike didn't mind the responsibilities of a teller. In fact, he actually liked some of them, the most obvious being flirting with the young female customers and, strangely enough, stamping the deposit receipts. As crucial as most elements of the job were, or so he was informed from his first day at the training session, printing the bank books after each transaction was recorded was important, particularly to customers who were retired or looked like they were about to retire.

Being a teller, albeit even a temporary one, gave him the opportunity to closely observe the customers, an activity that had grown to become another source for literary research and eventual literary composition. Perhaps, he thought, he could use his experience at the bank, as bland as advertised, to resurrect his writing career. It was a daydream, just like it was when he was in high school. As far as his relationship with Sharon was concerned, their estrangement never turned into anything legal, at least not then. Amazingly enough, the two of them were now getting along better than they did for years, in fact before they married, the principal proof the fact that they still made love like they had just met. Mike felt that if he told her about the recent reappearance of his literary daydreams, she would remind him about the major reason for her decision to ask him to leave their place on the top floor of that the damn Lamplighter apartment in the first place. He had to forget about the literary career.

The teller about whom he had developed a considerable infatuation, in fact it was more like an adolescent crush was named Susan. She was the classic California girl, blond, blue eyed, blessed with a delightfully cute button nose, a body that could have been designed by every adolescent boy from Frank Hardy to Dobie Gillis, the likely source of every fantasy prompted by every television show that featured a high school girl. Mike though didn't dare approach her in any meaningful way, not because he thought her haughty in any way but because she had a boyfriend named Salvatore, who may have struck fear in every male in the branch, even the manager Art Lawrence, who casually lusted after Susan like he did after almost every other female in the branch. Despite his limitations, as significant as they were, Mike did occasionally manage to attract Susan's notice, usually with an innocent stare that Susan might have thought endearing. So he was forced to pursue his crush, one of the few girls who was so qualified, going back to a young girl named Betty in grade seven, who he pursued by telephoning her practically every day for a month and hanging up if she answered.

Next to Susan's teller's station stood a woman named named Beverly who, while attractive enough herself, projected a threatening rather than innocent impression. Fact was that Beverly was commonly regarded, at least in the branch, as a slut, an unrepentant tramp as christened by Mr. Lawrence's secretary Marilyn. She was a woman who was married to a city bus driver named Ronny. The story of Beverly was that she would make love with pretty well any one who asked, including a rumoured predilection for women. Mike didn't believe most of the bank scuttlebutt, relying on the alternative view that she had earned her unsavory reputation, if that's what it was, because of her fashion sense, which was generally based on her opinion that any part of her anatomy that could be exposed should be, provided her outfits could be worn in nightclubs. Poor Beverly, thought Mike, to be called a slut or a stripper, take your pick. The four men who worked in the branch, whether it was the branch assistant manager Allan Smith, the short, pudgy Jim of the accounting section, the branch manager Art Lawrence and Mike himself, not to mention a woman or two, were all under the suspicion of having taken advantage of Beverly's charms, though everyone wondered who was taking advantage of whom.

The geometry of the tellers continued. There was Helen who was a large woman with enormous breasts and a caboose that rivaled that of a sumo wrestler. She was a competent teller who was often heard correcting or attempting to correct the other tellers, opinions that were contradicted by the head teller, who some people thought was a honorary post but really wasn't. She was an older woman, well dressed, well made up, her application of cosmetics appearing to be almost professional. Her name was Shirley and neither anyone in the branch nor anyone who had ever worked in the branch disagreed with the conclusion that Shirley was always right when it came to the business of being a bank teller. On the other hand, there was a certain sadness about Shirley that somehow suggested that she had suffered some unknown tragedy in her history, placing a look of crucifixion on her face. The last teller that Mike had to consider was Maureen who, despite Mike's infatuation with Susan and his short volcanic affair with her friend Beverly the slut, was something he eventually had to admit to himself, was the one teller, the one woman in the branch about whom he could have pursued an authentic romance. She was a tall, statuesque woman who always wore long dresses for reasons she never explained, at least not to him. It gave her a sophisticated appearance, as if she was the manager of an art gallery or a high end clothing store. Many in the branch often considered, if not questioned her choice in career, ruminating about a woman who certainly did not look the part of a bank employee.

The most important duty as a teller, arguably aside from serving the bank's customers, was to complete each working day with "accounts in balance". In other words, that your accounts, after a day of deposits, withdrawals, the purchase of certified cheques, loan and mortgage payments, paying utility bills and fees for safety deposit boxes, had to demonstrate that the amount of money you put out each day equaled the amount of money you took in. It was not any different than his daily duty at the Mint, what was put to work at the beginning of a shift, in terms of material, equaled what to gave back in terms of finished product at the end of the shift.

After a month of pretending to be a bank teller, he realized that his experience in the branch turned out to be much more memorable than his two years of labouring at the Mint. True, his tasks there were rudimentary to say the least. The place, which was a factory after all, was still noisy, dirty, and populated by men who for the most part offered Mike little in the way of interest and entertainment. Even after he was promoted to the position of shift supervisor, there was little to commend the Mint. Sure, there was the friends he made, the Mint sports teams on which he played, the comic vulgarity of most of his colleagues, the simplicity of the job itself, it posed no real difficulty, and the fact that Mike, at least during his term as midnight shift supervisor, could make extra money playing euchre or table tennis. On the other hand, he concluded that anytime you decide that your job embarrasses the hell of you, something like garbage collection or a position in the Canadian Senate, it is better to look elsewhere for a career. That and the offer by his wife to support his literary aspirations ultimately led him to the Bank of Montreal.

The next, and as it turned out the most permanent assignment at the bank was in the accounting section, five desks situated in a straight line to the right of the tellers and across the floor from Mr. Lawrence's office. At the head of the section that was accounting, was the desk of assistant manager of Allan Smith, a neatly attired man who supervised the bank's staff with the sure handed comportment of a school teacher. He always wore a three piece suit, a vest adorned with a silver watch fob, and a shirt and tie combination that added a finishing touch to his assistant bank manager costume. The bank manager Art Lawrence liked to refer to him as Bob Crachet, a characterization with which few, if any of the staff at the bank disagreed. While he was not popular with his colleagues in the branch, he was not disliked either, his colleagues sympathetic with his plight, however that may have been. The next most senior member of the management was the so-called head accountant, the supervisor of the accounting department, a stern looking, middle aged woman named Eleanor Warren. She conducted herself as if she was the head librarian, guiding her three subordinates with a firm hand. She was a large woman. Based on their comparative physical sizes, she made Allan Smith look like her adolescent son. She always had her graying hair in a tight bun. She usually wore a cardigan sweater over a white blouse, a flannel skirt of various colours, neutral support stockings and a pair of black walking shoes.

The desk right behind Miss Warren was occupied by an attractive young woman named Stephanie Murphy, who definitely did not look like she should be working in a bank. In addition, Mrs. Murphy was well dressed, leading to the impression that she used to be a fashion model or that her husband, a lawyer named Lance was exceptionally prosperous. It was definitely not congruent to imagine her sitting behind a desk, filling in forms, examining ledgers, directories, registers, and the like. In fact, and predictably, her formal position did not involve anything like that. It was entitled "Customer Service Representative", her responsibilities being to resolve issues for banking customers, most particularly lost credit cards, disputes over banking fees and the like, and any other complaints customers may have. It was surprising, therefore, that despite her apparent image, which would normally precipitate all sorts of envy among her colleagues, Mrs. Murphy was quite popular in the branch, not only the people who worked there but also the customers, many of whom usually chose to seek Mrs. Murphy's assistance rather than the assistance of another member of the accounting department who provided customers with assistance. Nelson often found himself ignored by customers seeking redress from whatever grievances they may have. On the other hand, the diminutive Mr. Nelson was also the branch's loan officer, reporting to both assistant manager Allan Smith and eventually branch manager Lawrence who was ultimately responsible for the issuance of loans and mortgage.

For the next eight months, Mike found himself mainly shuffling between the accounting department, teller's wickets,and loan processing, the latter position for which he was initially hardly qualified, a three day course in Montreal on loans and mortgages brought him some familiarity with the practice of lending people money which he was repeatedly told was the most important element of the banking business. Small wonder he thought given the complexity of the application form prospective candidates for a loan or a mortgage had to struggle through. In most ways, the forms resembled those employed by the tax department, giving the applicants the impression that they were not customers but sellers, attempting to convince the bank to lend them the money rather than attempting to convince the customers to borrow it. For this reason, Mike thought working the loan department was the most interesting of the jobs that he was asked to perform when he was in the employ of the bank.

Discussing applications for loans gave the bank officers the responsibility of investigating aspects of people's lives that would not normally be considered. Asking people about their jobs, their salaries, their expenses, personal details that would not normally be discussed by any customer who was not applying for a loan or a mortgage was probably disconcerting for anyone, including Mike who did not have any experience with prying into people's personal lives. While he had no such experience, he found that exploring the branch files regarding loans and mortgages was instructive, helpful in dealing with his future interviews with potential clientele. The files, which were secured in slate gray cabinets that were kept in the vault with the safety deposit boxes as was the cash that was used to sustain the branch. He did not think that he had authorization to explore the borrower files although he never asked. On the second day of his duties as an assistant loan officer, a title that loan officer Nelson conferred on him although Mike doubted that it had any official meaning but it made his supposed boss Nelson happy, he was informed by head teller Shirley Sutton that he might benefit from examining the loan files. In view of the fact that Miss Sutton was the longest serving employee of the branch, Mike had no doubts of the veracity of her suggestion. In the back of his mind, however, despite Miss Sutton's assurance, he thought that it would be unwise if he were to be discovered with the files.

So he began to carefully scrutinize the two file cabinets in the vault, removing the files one at a time and then concealing them in the bottom drawer of the desk in the accounting department. To avoid being discovered with a file, Mike would usually examine a file surreptitiously, either by covering it with an unrelated document or even bringing it home. Regardless of where he examined a file, he found some of them interesting, not all of them but some. Most of them were fairly predictable, accounts of assets, salaries, liabilities, that sort of thing. For the most part, despite his serious lack of experience with financial matters, Mike was able to understand the reasons for individual loan applications,whether they be automobile loans, credit card and other debts, costs of tuition, and any other expenses, no matter how unorthodox they seemed. In the latter regard, Mike couldn't believe some of the reasons that applicants were using to support their requests for a loan. On the other hand, applications for things like mortgages were pretty well self evident.

His fourth application had a man named John Wiseman requesting $15,000 to start what he called a "gentleman's club", which Mike immediately recognized was a strip club, the location of which was identified somewhere on the second floor of a building on Queen Street. He also recognized the building where Mr. Wiseman intended to open his "gentleman's club", a warehouse that overlooked a parking lot at the corner of Queen and Lyon Streets, across from the Sheraton Hotel. Mike read the rest of Mr. Wiseman's application with considerable curiosity. It was not surprising that the applicant sought a loan to open a "gentleman's club". It was apparent that he had worked in restaurants and nightclubs, not only in Ottawa but also in several nearby towns,specifically Carleton Place, Perth and Arnprior. As far as his current occupation was concerned, Wiseman indicated on the loan application that he had operated the Dominion tavern in the Byward market area and had for several years. As far as other details were concerned, Wiseman was divorced, had three children for which he paid support, owned two houses with sizable mortgages, paid loans on cars used by both him and his ex-wife and was leasing the Dominion tavern and much of its furniture and equipment. In addition, whoever had accepted Wiseman's loan application also indicated in the comment section of the form a negative observation, i.e. negative liability which, while Mike did not actually know what the comment meant, he had the general idea that Wiseman's loan application would likely be declined.

Aside from Wiseman's application, a week later he came across an application that made Wiseman look virtuous. This candidate for a loan, a man named Graham who had listed a number of jobs over the decade or so, admitted to declaring bankruptcy on at least two occasions over the period of time covered by his request for a loan, i.e. ten years. Still, most of the applications that Mike surveyed were almost identical to each other, stable middle class individuals with solid jobs, married with kids, the need for mundane ordinary things that everybody else had. Mike would wonder about the liabilities that his parents may have carried although he doubted they were burdened with much debt. In fact, both of them seemed to regard debt as some sort of punishment, something to be definitely avoided. So it was understandable that Mike had not borrowed any money up until then, although ever since he and Sharon broke up, he could have used a few bucks, particularly when he was between jobs.

It was his introduction to the filing cabinets that emerged as another important part of his experience as an assistant loan officer, as unofficial as the title may have been. There were two of the sheet metal monstrosities holding not only the loan applications but other documents relevant to the operation of the branch, including the records of all the accounts, both chequing and savings, the loans and mortgages, both current, closed and discontinued, receipts from fees from all sort of bank services, certified cheques, stop payments, travelers cheques, and safety deposit boxes. It was traditional that filing cabinets were vital to pretty well every workplace that involved the keeping of records. Even when Mike was working as a golf caddy, the "Caddy Master", would file the signed tickets that each caddy would submit after rounds of carrying golf clubs and the records of each payment made to the caddies who filed the tickets. Each position that he held after that first job maintained records and therefore held them in filing cabinets. Until he began working in the Mint though, he had not been responsible for anything that was filed in any cabinet, even though he had been aware of them ever since he first saw one since he first visited his father's office when he was five or six. They were always part of every place of work regardless of whether you were a bottom feeding clerk or an executive where you filed until your thumbs went numb.

The branch's filing cabinets, quietly secured in the back corner of the vault, looked like they were purchased from a company that had gone bankrupt. There were stickers affixed all over the two cabinets, suggesting somehow that they had been the target of some strange jibes that likely had not had anything to do with any kind of business that could have required a cabinet. It seemed entirely understandable therefore that the contents of both cabinets were as chaotic as the appearance of their external surfaces. Mike noticed that each application that he had examined was not chronologically filed, only two of the several dozens that he had studied were filed in any sort of order.

As a clerk, Mike was puzzled, if not surprised that no one had decided to organize the contents of the two cabinets in any orderly fashion. He asked his immediate boss Nelson why the files were not put in an organized way. Mr. Nelson simply shrugged.

Rather than recalling the various bureaucratic peculiarities that Mike's eleven months working at the branch revealed, Mike only recollected the social incidents that occurred during his working days at the branch. Sharon often commented that work days at the branch sounded more like a television soap opera than a place of business. Maybe once or twice a week, Mike would report on episodes that he thought worth relating, mainly due to their sexual nature. Almost all of them involved improper relationships between bank employees and between bank employees and bank customers. A primary source of salacious narratives would involve branch manager Art Lawrence who Mike often said had a profound predilection for harassing young girls, recently hired tellers his usual target. One of the most memorable incidents concerned an eighteen year old recent high school graduate named Cheryl who caught Mr. Lawrence's eye as soon as she visited the branch to apply for a position as a teller. She was talking to assistant manager Smith and head teller Shirley Sutton when manager Lawrence happened by, spotted Cheryl, and leaned down to interrupt the job interview. Within five minutes or less, Lawrence was conducting Cheryl into his office. She looked nervous. Head teller Sutton remarked that she looked like she was shy as a Quaker.

Several weeks later, after Cheryl had been hired as a teller, it became fairly obvious to everybody in the branch that Art Lawrence was pursuing the poor little Cheryl Bradley fairly hard. Many of her new co-workers were worried about her. After all, shy, inexperienced girls were not up to dealing with a philander like Art Lawrence. Some could and others couldn't, the latter group it seemed didn't last long in the employee of the Bank of Montreal. In Cheryl's case, she was would be called into Lawrence's office in the afternoon when there was little business, the door would be shut, the blinds in his office would be closed and Mr. Lawrence would tell his secretary Marilyn to hold his telephone calls. This was standard procedure with Mr. Lawrence's occasional girlfriends. Fifteen or twenty minutes later, Cheryl would leave the office, looking like she had been weeping, walking unsteady, her clothes slightly disheveled, she was noticeable. She would return to her wicket, still quietly weeping, a ball of tissues in her hands like she was holding a rosary. The other tellers pretended not to allow Cheryl's rendezvous with Mr. Lawrence to disrupt their work although every now and then, they would occasionally glance at head teller Sutton, implying somehow that she should have stopped Mr. Lawrence from harassing Cheryl Bradley. Although Miss Sutton did not take any immediate action to ameliorate Cheryl's distress, she did tell her to take the rest of the day off. She also recommended that she take the next day off as well. She did.

A week later, Mr. and Mrs. Bradley, Cheryl's parents, arrived at the branch for an appointment with Mr. Lawrence. It was ten o'clock in the morning and there were only five customers in the branch. Cheryl had been waiting for them, sitting in a chair by the desk of Mr. Lawrence's secretary Marilyn. Of the employees, only Marilyn and Shirley Sutton seemed to take notice of the Bradley parents. Cheryl rose from her chair and greeted her parents as did Marilyn who then escorted all three of them into Mr. Lawrence's office. He was waiting for the Bradleys by the door of his office. Their names were Harvey and Elaine and they were probably in their late forties or so. Lawrence greeted and then ushered them into the office. He offered his hand to the parents who declined to return the salutation. The three Bradleys sat on chairs in front of Lawrence's desk. Cheryl, however, moved her chair back a bit. It seemed appropriate to Lawrence somehow.

"I think you know why we're here." said Harvey, "Cheryl has been very upset since her, what would you call it, her meeting with you. When she told us what happened, at first we couldn't believe it, then we got very concerned. We think, in fact we know for sure, that our daughter wouldn't normally do what she did with you in your office that day." Lawrence leaned forward, his elbows on his desk, and replied to what could only be interpreted as an accusation, a serious accusation. "Your daughter Cheryl is a very attractive young lady and I was very attracted to her and she gave me the impression, the strong impression that she was attracted to me." At first, Harvey and Elaine Bradley both looked shocked. They then looked quietly enraged. He was now practically shouting. "And you thought it proper to molest my daughter in your damn office." Lawrence then stood up with both hands now on his desk and offered a defense of his actions, sort of. "I didn't molest her, I was trying to persuade her, seduce her. After a few minutes, I realized that she didn't have much experience. So I stopped." Elaine, who was not as angry as her husband, interjected, "That should not matter, ever, no matter who has experience or who doesn't. Besides, this is an office," she said, spreading her arms out in explanation."And you shouldn't persuade anything like that with anyone, particularly a young girl who works for you." Lawrence sat down and gestured toward the two of them to sit down as well. Mr. and Mrs. Bradley slowly joined him in taking their chairs. Their daughter had not moved since the three of them walked into the office. Now back behind his desk in a his chair, Lawrence then tried to offer an apology, as inadequate as it might have seemed. It was not accepted.

<hr>

The daughter of Harvey and Elaine Bradley resigned from her position as a teller at the Laurier & O'Connor Branch of the Bank of Montreal two days after her parents visited the office. It was understood that she transferred to a branch in the west end, a branch which was managed by a woman named Rebecca Laundry. Cheryl Bradley did not inform anyone of her departure, including head teller Shirley Sutton who had been her most ardent advocate through her five months working as a teller. On the other hand, Art Lawrence was not replaced as the manager of the Laurier & O'Connor Branch of the Bank of Montreal.

<hr>

His affair with Beverly lasted four months although it seemed at times to be somehow longer and at times somehow shorter. Amazingly enough, during their time together, Beverly did not pursue amorous activity with anyone else, including Ronny and his friends, a strange development given her history. They would pursue their adulterous acts at Mike's apartment pretty well every Tuesday evening when

Sharon was taking a business tutorial at Carleton University. In addition, they would meet for brief encounters in the second floor supply room the occasional afternoon although they took care to avoid using the space unless they were absolutely sure that no one else was either seeking supplies or using it for the same purpose as they were although the latter was never the case, at least as far as the two of them knew. While their evening meetings were somewhat relaxed, their supply room trysts lasted fifteen minutes at the most, a situation that required almost frenzied attention. Their preferred position used the only chair in the room. As a result, they would sometimes interrupt their amorous pursuits in the chair by falling out of it, a circumstance that sometimes precipitated laughter, which they would have to suppress lest they be discovered by the other occupants of the second floor of the building, a psychologist named Graham and his secretary. The only other danger was an article of clothing being left at the scene, an unlikely eventuality since the two of them seldom removed their clothing, maybe their underwear but little else.

Although it was long suspected, their affair was not actually discovered until Beverly's husband Ronny, the bus driver, appeared at the branch at ten thirty on a Friday morning in an evident rage. In a loud voice, he immediately sought the attention of his wife, who was serving a lady who was the first in a line of five other customers. It was obvious that everyone in the branch, most of the employees including manager Lawrence as well as maybe a dozen customers, were made immediately aware of the commotion. Ronny was holding a batch of papers in his left hand, yelling that he had found their love letters. "Which one is Mike?" Ronny demanded, a few moments later Mike himself was standing by Beverly presumably to protect, if not to comfort, her.

But before Ronny could get any closer to Beverly, he was maybe ten feet from Beverly's wicket when Mr. Lawrence intercepted him. Ronny stopped and then, in another loud utterance, ordered Beverly to come home with him that afternoon. He said that he would be by to pick her at three o'clock, an unexpected maneuver since Beverly usually took the bus, arriving home around five o'clock in the afternoon. For his part, her husband usually arrived home about six o'clock in the afternoon, his common practice to leave work around four o'clock, spend about an hour in a local tavern with his fellow bus drivers and then drive home. In other words, he never picked Beverly up at the branch at three o'clock in the afternoon or at any other time. Ronny the bus driver than left the branch after scattering the love letters on the counter of the accounting section, Beverly announced in a trembling voice that she would not be going home with her husband Ronny that day at three o'clock or any other time. She then asked her friend and fellow teller Susan if she could stay at her place until such time as she and Ronny could reconcile, if that was possible. She declined, answering that her boyfriend Salvatore would not agree to having Ronny's wife in their place. Susan told Beverly that Salvatore did not want to get involved in any sort of disagreement between husband and wife.

Before lunch, Mike had telephoned Sharon to explain the Beverly situation. He did not adequately describe his relationship with Beverly, only the danger she said she was in. Surprisingly, almost amazingly enough, Sharon actually agreed to Mike's proposal that the two of them shelter the anguished Beverly until things calmed down. He played the good Samaritan/hippie routine on Sharon, explaining that Beverly was afraid to go home, afraid that Ronny would beat her, a practice that he occasionally used during any spousal disagreement. Mike provided no further detail regarding the specific reason for Beverly's current anxiety although he was worried that his wife would somehow guess, thinking that maybe she already knew about their dalliance. Mike and Beverly arrived at the condominium off Carling Avenue area in the west end area of the city a little after five o'clock in the afternoon after taking a couple of buses from downtown. During the ride home, during which they held hands the entire way, Beverly repeatedly said that she couldn't believe that his wife had agreed to provide her sanctuary from her husband for a couple of days. For his part, Mike wanted to get an assurance from Beverly that her mother, who lived in Arnprior, had taken the kids. Beverly said that she was certain.

The evening was understandably curious. It seemed almost like a scene from a play that might have been seen played as a drama on television or in the Ottawa Little Theatre. Sharon and Beverly sat on the living room couch looking at Mike as if they both expected him to explain their circumstances to each other. Mike thought of Sharon meeting Beverly at the branch Christmas party and telling Mike in the car going home that she looked like a slut, a widely held opinion in the branch. For her part, Beverly said that she thought Sharon looked like she was not very good in bed. Mike did not comment.

They had dinner, had more than several drinks each, played records, watched television, and argued about whether Art Carney deserved to win an academy award for best actor as opposed to Jack Nicholson. Fact was that they discussed everything but the situation that was confronting them. All three of them turned in late. Just before midnight, all three were well on the edge of intoxication and ready to stumble toward slumber, Sharon and Mike to their bedroom and Beverly to the guest bedroom. Fortunately, it was a Friday night and they were looking forward to sleeping in. They probably felt that it would be necessary.

Around six o'clock the next morning, Ronny interrupted their expectations for extended sleep when he telephoned the Butler condo and asked for Beverly. He sounded sleepy and tearful. Mike, who had answered the call, told him that Beverly was asleep. Ronny began to rant, accusing Beverly and by implication Mike himself of ruining his family. Ronny then demanded that Mike wake her up immediately. Mike declined and attempted to encourage Ronny to calm down, telling him that he had his two children, two boys four and two, to think about. He thought he heard Ronny resume his tears. Meanwhile, Beverly had crept into the kitchen, knelt on the floor of the kitchen, grasped his morning erection which she had removed from his underwear bottoms and began to stroke it. Mike stepped back and shook his head.

After that Friday, Beverly never appeared again as a teller or in any other function in the Laurier & O'Connor Branch of the Bank of Montreal. On the following Monday, Manager Lawrence gathered the entire staff fifteen minutes before the branch opened at ten o'clock to announce that Beverly Callahan had resigned from her position as a teller. The supposition was that Beverly had finally concluded that it was time to abandon Ronny, the latest display of marital discord on the past Friday the crucial and final episode. It came as no surprise that most of her now former co-workers said that Beverly's decision to dismiss her husband was long overdue. Head teller Sutton was quoted frequently after she observed, with an obvious cliché, that Beverly's decision was "long overdue". Everybody in the branch agreed with that sentiment.

No one knew where she went, even her friend Susan didn't know. The most generally accepted speculation was that she took her two boys and moved in with her mother in Arnprior. But maybe two weeks later, Mike thought he saw Beverly on a bus going down Queen Street. It was rush hour and the bus was crowded. Beverly was standing up by the back door. That was the last time he saw her.

A CAREER DELAYED AGAIN

He could not quite explain it but he decided to leave his position at the bank at the end of August. He had been considering the move for some time although he could not tell himself, let alone anyone else, when it began. He requested a few minutes with manager Art Lawrence on a Monday morning. It was a little after nine o'clock in the morning and Mr. Lawrence had been going through the mail. He waved Mike in and gestured him toward one of the chairs in front of his desk. Mike sat down and immediately provided Lawrence with the reason for his visit.

"I've been thinking a lot about my career with the bank. I thought I would share my thoughts about that with you. I was thinking about talking with Allan but decided that talking with you might be more appropriate."

Lawrence looked at Mike with a casual, almost bored expression on his face. He had experience with listening to trainees contemplating their futures. It was natural, normal. Towards the end of their training, they all began to worry about what the bank had in store for them in the future. "What's on your mind, Mike?" asked Lawrence, even though he though he knew.

Mike smiled and replied. "I've been thinking about

my future and I've decided it's not with the bank. I should apologize to the bank for wasting the training over the past year or so but I've concluded that banking just isn't for me."

Lawrence leaned back in his chair and looked a little surprised. He was not exactly prepared for Mike's admission but asked the logical question anyway. "Are you resigning?"

He had informed Sharon of his decision to abandon his career in banking on the evening after he had informed Mr. Lawrence. He had originally planned to tell Sharon of his decision before he told Lawrence but was worried that she would talk him out of quitting. That evening, he said that he wanted to return to writing, an ambition he had temporarily given up after failing to attract a publisher more than a year ago. That decision resulted in his pursuit of a career in banking, which was basically the most attainable profession that a man in his mid-twenties without any qualifications to speak of could secure. But, after eleven months of learning how dull banking could be, he came to the conclusion that wherever the Bank of Montreal planned to assign him after his training was complete, he would be dissatisfied. So with maybe a couple of weeks left before somebody from regional headquarters would tell him to which branch he would be permanently transferred to, he decided to resume his literary career. He thought, without any basis he later discovered, that Sharon would not likely object, her job even more prosperous than it was when he had quit the Mint a couple of years before. In fact, in the months since Beverly spent the night at the Butlers' condominium, Mike had moved with Sharon to a penthouse apartment downtown although Mike himself was not consulted in any way about the move.

They were ensconced in the penthouse apartment maybe a month when Mike told her he planned to leave his position at the bank. He could not but should have anticipated her response. She looked at him, eyes in a cold stare, standing there in a firm posture, and then told him that she no longer saw any purpose in maintaining their relationship. It was not a coincidence although it might have been. Over the past several weeks, if not months, the two of them had had little to do with each other. Sharon had earned another promotion, Mike therefore thinking that Sharon would be in a better position than she was previously to support his writing. But he could not have been more wrong. Sharon, however, had replied negatively, decidedly disinterested in not only supporting his literary ambitions but his daily life as well. Sharon told him, in fact ordered him in a remarkably casual tone of voice to collect his belongings, mainly his two three piece suits, a half a dozen tailored collared shirts, a few ties, a dozen t-shirts, underwear, shoes, coats and several plastic milk cartons of record albums, and depart what used to be theirs but was now was plainly hers and hers alone.

This time, she gave him two weeks and she had not been drinking. She sounded like she had memorized her statement beforehand, which was basically what it was. It was like she was reading a line of dialogue from a movie.

With his resignation from the bank and his wife's apparent resignation from their marriage, Mike now faced two complications which he would have to settle. He now needed a place to live and presumably a job although he could probably survive on unemployment insurance if he could manage to scrape enough to get by for the eight week waiting period. He first thought of asking Sharon for a loan or better still a gift of maybe a couple hundred dollars. After all, he was not exactly flush, his bank account containing $82 and his pocket containing another $28 and some change. After Sharon had given him notice, he sat in the living room for a while watching television and contemplating his circumstances. While there was no doubt in his mind that he would apply for unemployment insurance as soon as he could, he would have to wait at least eight weeks before getting any benefits.

He started to look through the classified advertisements in the newspapers the next morning. The previous evening, as he was laying next to Sharon with whom he had just had sex, a kind of valediction, he returned to the point of panic about his financial situation. The way he calculated it, he would exhaust his funds within three weeks, if not sooner. Further, it would require eight weeks before he could expect an unemployment insurance payment. And more importantly, he would have to rent an apartment, without money and without a job, being left to living in a bachelor apartment in a derelict dump for less than $100 a month, like he had when he first arrived in Ottawa several years ago. So he concluded that he had no choice but to find employment, preferably a position that would pay him more than $2.40 an hour, the minimum wage at the time. It reminded him of the situation he faced several years ago when he left university.

It was almost a miracle of good fortune when Mike came across a small notice in the classified section of the *Ottawa Citizen* the next day advertising a job vacancy at a car rental agency several blocks away from the apartment building from which he was recently asked to leave. The position was entitled "customer service clerk" and described its tasks in three basic lines: greeting customers, renting them cars or trucks, and ensuring that the cars or trucks were returned in a timely fashion. He decided he would drop by the agency, which was called the Ottawa Car Rental, an uninspiring name to say the least, on Bank Street on his way home.

It was almost five o'clock when he arrived at the agency. There was a customer handing in the key to a rental car he was returning. Accepting the key was the other "customer service clerk", an attractive woman in her thirties with whom the customer returning the rental car was vigorously flirting. Her name was Cindy. The woman was laughing at practically every word the gentleman was saying and occasionally touching the sleeve of his jacket. Mike waited by the door. After a couple of minutes, the customer left, passing him out the door with a wave to the woman and a curious little nod to Mike who then quickly stepped up to the counter and told her that he was there to apply for the position of "customer service clerk", a statement that elicited a quiet giggle from the woman who was presently holding that job. He then introduced himself as Mike Butler.

"Hello, Mike, my name is Cindy. Mr. Brennan, there's a man here who wants to apply for a job like mine." the woman directing her announcement over her shoulder towards the closed office behind her. She then looked at Mike and told him that Mr. Brennan, who he presumed was the boss, would probably be right out. She then looked at him with a certain semi-serious expression on her face and asked in a soft tone, almost as if she was actually interested in the answer. "Are you sure you want to apply for this position? I mean, it's a pretty boring job." With that admission, she smiled and expanded on that characterization. "I've been here six months and the most exciting part of this job is when Mrs. Brennan comes in to go over the books." Mike smiled and understandably asked with a hint of levity, "How could that be exciting? Why, does she examine the books naked or something?" With that, Cindy's smile grew into a laugh. "No, nothing like that. You see, anytime she comes in, she ends up accusing her husband of not knowing what he is doing, calling him stupid, dumb and stuff like that, and threatens to start coming in everyday to manage the place." Cindy then went on to explain that Mrs. Brennan's father owned the place and when he passed away, she got the business. Cindy had proceeded to whisper. "She made Mr. Brennan the manager. Mr. Brennan was the damn mechanic for god's sake and maybe not a very good one. I guess Mrs. Brennan thought she had to do it. Or something like that."

Mr. Brennan, a corduroy brown fedora sitting on his head like some sort of weird exclamation mark, then appeared from behind the office door. He looked a little annoyed, which according to Cindy and later to the current mechanic, a guy named Dan, and most of the customers, was his normal expression. Further, it didn't seem to change much as Cindy introduced Mike to him as a job applicant. Mike provided Brennan with an embarrassed smile, offered his hand and introduced himself. Brennan ignored Mike's hand and observed, "I guess you saw the ad in the paper, right?" Mike nodded and added an explanation, which was probably unnecessary. "Yes, I saw it and I want to apply. I came over as soon as I could." Brennan looked at him, his annoyance now replaced with a blank look on his face. He then moved closer and slid a blank piece of paper and a pen across the surface of the counter. "I'll just need your full name and telephone number." Mike picked up the pen, compiled with Brennan's request and pushed the paper back to Brennan. He then stared at Brennan and asked an obvious question. "Is that all you want to know? ", the absence of a request for any other information, say on a standardized form, a startling development. Mike just stood there with a bewildered look on his face. Cindy, who had been standing behind Brennan, shrugged her shoulders and noted, "He just asked me my name, didn't even ask me to write it down."

Brennan reacted with a perverse little smile, turned to look at Cindy and observed. "And it worked out, didn't it?" Cindy followed with another giggle. Not as pronounced as before but heard nonetheless, she agreed with Brennan. "I've been here for six months and I haven't had any problems with any paperwork." Brennan's smile broadened a bit and he assured Mike that he didn't need any further information. "Look, give me a day or so, I'll see if there are any more applications and then I'll let you know."

<hr />

Mike started at the Ottawa Car Rental on the following Monday, convenient timing since the previous Friday was his last day at the bank. Brennan was to pay Mike $4.00 an hour, which amounted to about $150.00 a week, which was slightly less than the $8,500 annually he was making as a management trainee at the Bank of Montreal. But it was employment, nothing that could be regarded as a way towards a possible career he knew but it would support him as he pursued a literary vocation, that is if he still could.

That first day, Cindy, who was wearing her usually indecent outfit, a low neck sweater and a skirt that looked like it could have been worn by an adolescent girl auditioning for a bad reputation, educated Mike on the complexities of the store's rental contracts, a document that all potential renters had to complete. She also repeated manager Brennan's instruction that all customers had to be appropriately appraised for their financial bona fides. In other words, "customer service clerks" must make certain that the people renting the cars would return them. As previously advised, the most likely manner in which the financial stability of anyone applying to rent a car was the possession of a valid credit credit. As Brennan must have told him a dozen times, the acceptance of cash or cheques would require scrutiny to determine whether the customer was trustworthy and their credit good. Cindy thought that most customers who didn't have a credit card were probably not creditworthy anyway but said that Brennan was usually reluctant to pass up a sale.

So, even though every other "customer service clerk" who ever worked in the Ottawa Car Rental probably agreed that such potential customers may not be worth the effort of vetting them, they continued to interrogate customers that didn't have credit cards lest they lose the rental or lose the car. Cindy made every effort to avoid dealing with the insolvent, meaning that it was left to Mike to deal with every customer who may have had financial shortcomings. Most of them, although there weren't that many of them, were agreeable enough, then evasive, then even angered when asked for the details of their finances. After experiences with several such customers, nearly all of which were unpleasant, Mike had a sudden notion, drafting a short questionnaire regarding their financial situation. He thought that requesting an applicant to complete a questionnaire rather than being subjected to some sort of interview was less likely to cause discomfort for them. Mike was correct. Some customers were mildly annoyed, most weren't. Although he never gave Mike any reason, Mr. Brennan did not approve of Mike's questionnaire. He did not, however, prohibit him from continuing to ask customers to fill in his financial questionnaire. Even Cindy also began to employ the questionnaire although she tried to avoid such customers.

Mike met the soon to be most important client of the Ottawa Car Rental one morning around nine when Mr. Brennan had been late for work. He was a middle aged business man who introduced himself by handing Mike a business card that identified him as Jeffrey Dover, assistant manager of Ottawa operations for Bell Canada. Mike had the impression that Mr. Dover thought that he should have known who Dover was. In any event, Mr. Dover informed Mike that he had an appointment to meet with Mr. Brennan who then conveniently came in through the front door to greet him. Dover extended his hand, Brennan shook it, and handed him a document, several pages which the latter identified as the contract, presumed by Mike to be an agreement between Bell Canada and Ottawa Car Rental. In accepting the contract, Mr. Dover responded, "I trust I will find the terms of the contract to be satisfactory, consistent with our recent discussions." Brennan nodded and assured Dover that someone, who he introduced as Mike Butler, would be there every weekday to pick up whichever Bell Canada employee needing a rental car for that day. Cindy, who was standing by Mike at the counter and had been gazing shamelessly at Mr. Dover, her customary approach to any male who looked approachable, added that she would be occasionally on pick up duty herself, a responsibility that prompted her to a spasm of the giggles.

Dover placed the document on the counter, leaned in and started to read the contract. Brennan stood looking at Dover for several minutes. He then made what he thought would be a helpful comment. "If you see any problems with the contract, Mr. Dover, we can get our lawyer down here anytime we need him." Dover looked up, somewhat annoyed and questioned Brennan in a brusque manner. "Expecting a problem?" Brennan looked surprised and a little self-conscious, as if he was embarrassed by the possibility that anyone would find something wrong with the contract, which was appraised by more than one lawyer in the firm retained by Mrs. Brennan. "No, no, I can assure you that our lawyers have gone over the contract a few times." Mr. Dover smirked a bit, still looking a little annoyed and went back to scrutinizing the contract. Mike, who had been loitering in the rear of the office, approached the counter as another customer came through the office door. Brennan then suggested that he and Dover complete their consultations in the former's private office. Dover agreed and then, with a surprising smile, asked that Cindy, who had been smoking a cigarette with the mechanic in the shop's garage to accompany the two of them to Brennan's office. When requested, Cindy giggled and seemed to almost skip into the office. Brennan seemed completely dumbfounded while Dover was wearing a smug grin. They both followed Cindy into Brennan's office and then closed the door. mike could not avoid hearing laughter coming from the office. Brennan was serving them drinks. That was one thing he was good at.

* * *

A little more than six months after he started at the Ottawa Car Rental Mr. Brennan called him into his private office and told him that he could no longer afford to employ Mike. In effect, he was being laid off. He said that he would pay Mike the customary two weeks severance, the amount of which he could not determine. Cindy, with whom he had initiated and was still pursuing an affair, one or two sessions a week the norm, was let go almost a month before. After Cindy was laid off, her reaction to the decision nonchalant if not welcoming, mechanic Dan told Mike that after letting both Cindy and himself go, Brennan and the family, his wife and two teenage children, both of whom thought their father was a dolt, went on vacation for three weeks. When Brennan returned, two new "customer service clerks" were hired, Brennan's brother-in-law Nolan having recruited them, presumably for maybe another six months. Dan said that this was Brennan's pattern over the past five years, which was the length of Dan's employment at the Ottawa Car Rental. As for Dan, he got a three week vacation.

Strangely or ironically or coincidentally, Cindy and Mike never made love again after he was let go. There was, however, the occasional tryst with his soon-to-be ex-wife Sharon. On the other hand, it only happened a couple of times.

UIC AVOIDED
WHITE COLLARS
MAY SEEM BLUE

With an additional week's pay as severance and a perfunctory adieu, Mike Butler said farewell to the Ottawa Car Rental on the last day of March, almost exactly six months after he first began his employment there. As his final act, he had rented a Chevrolet Impala to a man named Kelly, who said that he wanted the car for a weekend trip to Toronto. Dan the mechanic, who gave him a bottle of cheap Scotch as a going away gift, asked him what he intended to do now that he was out of work, again as Mike had pointed out. He thought about it for a moment, as he had for several days before that, and said that he had decided that he once again would apply for unemployment insurance, a familiar sanctuary when he did not have a job, which was almost occasional. Now it was a Friday. He would visit the UIC office on Carling Avenue on Monday and fill in an application.

Prompted perhaps by Dan's gift of a bottle of cheap Scotch, Mike spent most of following weekend intoxicated, inebriated, almost completely drunk, and in the words of a college friend named Larry, besotted. He managed to clear his head long enough by Saturday afternoon to visit the Metro grocery store on Bank Street to pick up some food and other provisions, specifically aspirin and something to settle his stomach. On his way back to his place on Frank Street, as he was swallowing as much antacid as he could to calm his turbulent tummy, he ran into a former colleague, a guy named Ray Kramer with whom Mike had been fairly friendly when they both worked in the Mint. They both recognized each other almost immediately, even though Kramer had grown a beard and was now wearing his hair longer than Mike recalled. He assumed that Kramer no longer worked in the Mint, which had moved to Winnipeg since he saw him last. Mike never even bothered asking where he was now working, assuming that he was, although he volunteered that he had just been let go from his job at a crummy car rental. Kramer laughed and said that he knew the feeling, having had a couple of jobs since he had decided not to take the offer of a transfer to Winnipeg. "I was thinking of going with the Mint to Winnipeg but my wife, who was pregnant at the time, didn't want to live in Winnipeg. So I declined their offer, took my severance and decided to take UIC for a while." Mike nodded and asked about this current job. "I'm working on the line for the bank note company. It's kind of funny, working for the Mint and now the Canadian Bank Note Company. It's not so bad, better than the Mint, and certainly better than looking for another job. So what are you going to do?" Mike spread his arms out, gave Kramer a quick grin and explained his plans. "I thought I would go on UIC for a while." Then they both smirked.

It was several months later that Mike was notified by telephone that he had to appear for a meeting at the UIC office on Carling Avenue. At that meeting, he was informed that he had a couple of months to secure gainful employment, no matter how depressing the prognosis, or face a charge of criminal fraud, a dreadful prospect that scared the hell of him. The threatened charge was due to making specious claims to the Unemployment Insurance Commission (UIC), the government agency that decades ago had made not having a job less embarrassing than it may have been in the past. Specifically, the false assertions he had allegedly made involved informing the agency, in writing mind you, that he had applied for positions when in fact he had not, statements that were easily verified as prevarications. Apparently, in order to receive unemployment benefits, one had to provide evidence of actively looking for work, a requirement that he had ignored without regret.

So when he was advised by an official during an interview at the UIC office that not only were his benefits to be immediately terminated, leaving him significantly short of cash, but he could face criminal charges, he panicked. His reaction was understandable, if not predictable. At first, he foolishly contemplated suicide but eventually settled on getting drunk with a friend who fortunately had recently graduated from UIC to welfare. Faced with obtaining immediate employment, which the threatening UIC official had indicated was his only way out of his current quandary, he decided that obtaining a temporary clerical position with the tax department, a job that he understood was always available for workers desperate enough to take it, was his most likely choice.

So he took the city bus down Bank Street to the Billings Bridge shopping centre and then walked over to the tax department on Heron Road. He entered the building, which officially housed the Canada Revenue Agency, and asked the receptionist at the desk by the door to direct him to the personnel office. The receptionist, who happened to be a uniformed commissioner, pointed to the elevators to the right, and told Mike that personnel was on the second floor. There he stood before another receptionist although this one, a middle aged woman, was not wearing a commissionaire uniform but a black pant suit. She looked up from whatever it was that she was studying and asked about his business. Mike said that he was there to apply for a temporary position reviewing tax forms. The woman, who was introduced by the nameplate on her desk as Joan Hughes, handed him an application form, told him to have a seat to her left, and said that someone would be out to talk to him shortly.

It was a mercifully and surprisingly short job application, befitting Mike thought the significance, or lack thereof of the importance of the job to which it referred. He filled it in and handed it back to Joan Hughes and returned as directed to the seat to her left. She told him to wait and said that someone would be with him shortly. Mike sat in a chair as directed and waited, staring at a blank wall until a slightly harried but cheerful looking younger man arrived in the room. He picked up Mike's application for employment from Mrs. Hughes' desk, walked up to Mike and introduced himself. "I'm Allan Chambers, you're Mike Butler and you're looking for a temp job, right?" Mike nodded and stood up to shake Mr. Chambers' hand. "Yes, I am. I need a job and this seems to fit." Chambers smiled and started to examine Mike's application. After a few moments, Chambers looked up after his perusal of Mike's application. "I don't know why we ask people to fill in these applications. I mean, as I'm sure you probably figured out by now, practically anyone can do this job though most of our successful candidates are either college students or people like you, you know, people looking for any work, even if it's temporary." Mike nodded.

Chambers then outlined the job, which hardly needed much of an explanation."You would be filling information provided by individual taxpayers into a computer program which would then calculate that person's taxes." Mike then explained the surprised look on his face. "I've never worked on a computer before, I wouldn't know how." It was Chambers' turn to nod and smile. "I don't think you'd have to worry about that. It would take maybe half an hour to learn how to fill in the information. It won't be difficult. I should tell you though that we have a quota system." Predictably, Mike responded with a question. "A quota system! What does that mean?" Chambers answered quietly. "Well, if anybody can't process enough tax returns within a certain time period, that person would be dismissed. The other condition of the job that you should know is that if we don't have enough returns on any given day, then staff will be asked to stay home ----- and unfortunately, they wouldn't be paid for that day."

Mike was told that he could start a temporary position as a "tax processing clerk" the next day under the conditions outlined by Allan Chambers. He was to be paid $3.50 an hour, the lowest wage that he had received in several years.

The next day, after again reporting to the personnel department on the second floor where he signed a couple of forms, he reported to the tax processing section. It was nine in the morning. It was a large room with eight rectangular tables at which six chairs were placed at each one. He was greeted at the head of the room by a middle aged man who looked like he had slept in his clothes. His name was Bill. He had three associates, all of whom looked like they were just out of high school. They were pushing metal carts carrying tax returns around the room while thirty clerks sat before computer monitors and accepted them for processing. Most of the clerks, which were more or less divided between genders, looked like they were in their twenties, the only exceptions being three men, all of whom seemed to be in their thirties. None of them looked like they were down on their luck, which was the condition that Mike expected. One of them looked like a university professor, either that or an artist. As he later discovered, the man, whose name was Quinn, was not only an artist but a jazz musician as well. Everybody was casually dressed.

The job was almost absurdly simply. He was to transfer each individual figure on every return to the computer. The computer program would then calculate the taxes or refunds owed to each taxpayer based on his or her return. The production of each clerk in terms of the number of returns processed would then be accessed in the context of the required quotas and clerks would be either retained or let go. Judgments based on the quotas would then be made at the end of each week and processing clerks would be returned or be seeking alternate employment the next week. Allan Chambers had told him during his brief interview the previous Friday that twenty percent of the clerks who were ever hired continued into the second week and another twenty percent made it into the third week. In addition, Chambers said that almost fifty percent of the clerks hired made it three months, which was usually the standard term for the processors, at least in most years according to Chambers.

Mike found the atmosphere, as tedious as the work was, fairly pleasant given the circumstances. First of all, the room seemed to be populated by a fairly cheerful group, which could have been expected given that most of the clerks were either in university or just out of high school. On top of that, a good part of the obviously ebullient coterie seemed to be college girls, which of course enthused the hell out of Mike in particular. By the time he was in his third week, he had an interest in at least two of his female colleagues and at least one other female colleague seemed to have an interest in him. All four of the female colleagues who could be involved in some sort of relationship with him, you could call them dalliances or potential dalliances, appeared to be around twenty years old. One of them, the one in which he had developed the most serious infatuation, was an extremely attractive, well dressed university student who was doubtlessly more sophisticated, if not smarter than her fellow colleagues in the room, if not the entire building. Her name was Carole. Mike could not quite figure out how a woman like Carole ended up working as a temporary office clerk for the tax department. Still, despite the fact that he was intimidated by Carole, he made efforts, however awkward, to get acquainted with her. And over the next few weeks, he was successful.

Donna, the other woman in whom Mike had an interest, or thought he had an interest, however superficial it may have been, was generally regarded around the room as flirtatious, if not verging on the promiscuous. Unlike

Carole, Donna appeared to be comparatively naive, a girl barely out of high school, a young girl who wore cheaply provocative clothes, including extremely short skirts, applied cosmetics obviously purchased in a pharmacy, and conducted herself in a manner that endeavored to make her alluring to practically every male around her. Without a doubt and despite his best judgment, Mike was attracted to her, the hope of a seduction high on his wish list. He therefore spent some of his spare work time, of which there was plenty given his quota standing, slipping her an occasional glance, wistful looks that he thought might somehow lead to some sort of seduction. Donna definitely seemed to react positively, smiling shyly every time Mike looked at her. On the other hand, Mike was discretely sneaking glances at Carole as well although she did not seem to take any notice of them. Besides, she was seated three rows ahead of him while Donna was conveniently seated only one row behind.

Seated beside Donna was a girl named Maria who some of his male colleagues advised him to avoid, suggesting that she was seriously infatuated with him, observing that she would stare at him incessantly during both lunch and break periods. It was rumoured among some of her colleagues, most particularly her friends, that Maria was counseled to abandon her crush on Mike, claiming that following him after work was not a particularly good way to charm Mike or anybody else for that matter. Mike was embarrassed and a little troubled by Maria's apparent attention. Quinn, the artist/musician with whom he had struck up a fairly substantial friendship, thought Maria's infatuation for him quite humorous, reminding him, he said, of things that happened in elementary school. Quinn's observation about Maria and elementary school conjured for Mike, at least for a moment, a memory of his first girlfriend, who used to escort him by force to school when they both were in grade two. Ironically, maybe several weeks later, Mike attended a party at Quinn's place, a two bedroom basement apartment in an old building on Elgin Street, where he met his girlfriend, a nineteen year old who looked like a model. Further and surprisingly, Quinn suggested to Mike that he ask Carole to the party. That evening, he and Carole were to start a romantic relationship which was to last for several months, even after their employment at the tax department was over. Fortunately, by the time Carole and Mike had begun their affair, Maria had given up on any sort of amorous entanglement with Mike.

***

Mike was unemployed again, his third such sentence in the previous five years. In view of his experience with the UIC office on Carling Avenue, most specifically the threat of being arrested for fraud, he decided that he would start applying for another job as soon as he could rather than applying for UIC benefits. He was concerned that his name was on some sort of list of delinquent recipients of UIC benefits. Practically everyone with whom he had discussed his dilemma, including both Carole and Quinn, both of whom had plans that did not involve applying for another job, advised him against attempting to receive UIC again. In studying the want ads of the *Ottawa Citizen* the following Monday, he came across several notifications of agencies which hired workers for temporary positions. After contemplating the possibility, he concluded that the only thing he could do in the current circumstances and on such short notice was a temporary job through one of the employment agencies listed in the paper.

He was interested in several of the jobs listed, temporary clerical positions, the duties being to monitor the efficiency of clerical staff in government departments by recording their individual job related activities. The next day, he visited the office of the "Temporary Services Ltd.", a personnel agency on Albert Street. The first position that he came across was tacked to a cork board above the receptionist sitting in front of the elevator on the third floor. The job was advertised as "An Efficiency Surveillance Clerk". Mike stood in front of the receptionist's desk and asked about the job, for which he had already decided to apply. The receptionist, who was unnamed, no name plate or any other identification visible, handed Mike a laminated sheet on which the position was described. Mike then requested an application which was dutifully handed over by the receptionist who then provided him with a dirty look. Mike said he would return in fifteen minutes, no spare chairs being available in the office. He went down to a coffee shop on the ground floor to complete the form, swallowed a cup of coffee and was back to hand it to the receptionist with the disapproving look in less than the fifteen minutes as promised. The receptionist accepted the form and said, "Someone will be in touch with you presently". Mike thanked her, surprised by the term she had used.

Later that day, he received a telephone call from an avuncular sounding Mr. Conrad, who was to Mike a complete opposite to the ill-mannered disposition of the receptionist. He was told to report to the 15th floor of the Jean Mance Building in Tunney's Pasture on Scott Street. He was to work for Heath Canada, overseeing the work of twelve clerks and secretaries, all of whom would be subject to efficiency surveillance. In short, he had become an efficiency expert, an ironic function for a man who had been paid to be inefficient in many of his previous positions. The activities he monitored, aside of course from lunch, were to include filing, typing, talking on the telephone, talking to co-workers or talking to themselves, adding up numbers, attending meetings, avoiding meetings, making excuses, taking coffee breaks, taking washroom breaks, daydreaming, gazing thoughtlessly at nothing, or contemplating quitting their job entirely. He would walk from desk to desk, carrying a clipboard and recording job activities on a spreadsheet that looked suspiciously like an abstract painting. He was understandably not very popular with his subjects. In fact, most of whom regarded him with almost total disdain. Raised middle fingers were particularly popular.

On the other hand, he was able to flirt with some of those subjects, at least one in particular. Her name was Diane. She wore glasses and looked like a librarian. Despite an indication of an adventurous side, having confided to him at one point that she sometimes didn't wear underwear, she also seemed depressed somehow, giving him the quiet impression that she seemed to have failed somehow in her ambition, whatever that was. He thought that Diane might have looked suicidal at times and sometimes expressed a certain complaint about her lowly position in Health Canada, blaming the ignominy of her job as a lowly government clerk on the fact that she couldn't afford to attend to university. He did not record this fact on his spreadsheet.

He and Diane went out a couple of times, both times to a jazz club in the market. They ended up sleeping together although their relationship, understandably casual it may have been, only lasted as long as his tenure at Heath Canada.

Nominally in charge of the clerical surveillance group was a short bespectacled man who wore the same clothes every day and looked like he was suffering from a permanent hangover. His name was Bill Barnes and said that he used to work in a bank but admitted, almost boasting about it, that he was now on parole after serving time for some sort of financial transgression. Most people in the office, however, considered the claim absurd, many observing that Mr. Barnes would have trouble robbing a vending machine. It came as no surprise then that Bill Barnes was easy to work for. He didn't seem to be concerned with the efficiency of the three people who were working for him, another incongruity in a list of curious inconsistencies that seemed to characterize him. He was reporting on efficiency but did not seem to care about the efficiency of the people compiling the information that would go into that report, particularly in the afternoon when he was seldom seen, the suggestion was he spent the afternoon relaxing in a tavern on Somerset Street. It was no surprise then that at least two of the people who were supervised by Mr. Barnes, he and a woman named Claire basically ignored Barnes and his instructions, often handing in reports that were mostly fictitious, their spreadsheet entries invented on the spot. The third member of Barnes' staff was an older woman, possibly the oldest individual on the floor. He and Claire both thought that she was actually taking her responsibilities seriously, not that Bill Barnes would notice either way. He wondered whether anyone at "Temporary Services Ltd." would notice.

TEMPORARY NO MORE

A s expected, the Health Canada assignment had been short term casual assignment. From there, the agency hired him for another short term casual assignment to another government department, named Industry, Trade & Commerce (ITC), a large department which was then in the process of physically relocating into a new building on the corner of Bank and Queen streets in downtown Ottawa. The place was called the C.D. Howe Building, named after a former Liberal Cabinet Minister who was known as the "Minister of Everything" during most of the 1950's. Mike was hired as an import permit clerk, sitting at a huge table in the middle of the tenth floor with maybe two dozen other clerks. He was making $5.00 an hour. He worked four or five days a week, depending on the number of permit applications that needed to be processed. He also knew that he could be laid off at any time, the main reason to hire people from a personnel agency in the first place. Most of his colleagues at that table were from other agencies, the remaining clerks being full time employees who seemed to Mike to have graduated from being lazy to being entirely useless. One could always identify the latter. There were the ones who never did anything, sitting at the table, smoking, reading newspapers, and occasionally sneaking a drink from a coffee cup that did not contain coffee. They were untouchable it seemed, a strong union the apparent explanation.

Due to a change in government policy regarding certain import regulations, which resulted in a requirement for additional permit clerks in a certain section of ITC, Mike was fortunate enough to advance from casual employment to short term and then permanent clerical positions. It took Mike less than a year to achieve promotions that would have otherwise taken him at least several years. In addition, it would eventually provide him with another chance at a career. The history of Mike's ascent was understandably memorable.

<hr />

The first day at the permit office was on the second Monday in November of 1976. He was one of several clerks starting that day. All of them were retained by different personnel agencies, all presumably offering the clerks who started that day the same conditions of employment. He was assigned to the clothing permit section, joining a dozen other clerks scrutinizing permit applications to determine whether the applicant had filled in the form properly and had the appropriate quota. Aside from two or three permanent clerks, who because of their status could not be arbitrarily fired and therefore were often indolent, the table was populated by a variety of people who were otherwise unemployed and were working for various personnel agencies. It seemed like most of them were smoking and drinking coffee although it was suspected that not all of them were drinking coffee out of the coffee cups, liquor bottles hidden in their coats and backpacks. In addition, a majority of the clerks were frequently using expletives, only the two females at the table seemingly disturbed by the bad language. Their supervisor, a stern looking, matronly woman named Helen, would walk by the table every thirty minutes or so to monitor the clerks, mainly to collect the applications that had been handled and answered any questions any of them may have had. The clerks suspected that Helen's main job was to count the number of approved applications and therefore import permits to be issued. The clerks who were somehow delinquent in completing the appropriate number of applications were dismissed and then possibly let go by whatever agency that had hired them in the first place. In the few weeks that he sat at that table assessing import permit applications, at least half a dozen agency clerks were discharged.

Mike was released as well but not out of ITC but to another section that issued import permits covering products other than clothing. In this case, it was footwear, a recently determined policy change due, as Mike overheard in the tenth floor washroom, to the diminished footwear manufacturing in the province of Quebec in particular. In the meantime, the table accommodating the clerks handling import permit applications for clothing was dispersed and its clerks transferred to other sections or returned to their agencies. One of the clerks who had worked with Mike at the table was also transferred to the footwear section, a woman named Joyce. The manager of the new section, who was a long serving officer who had been working in the import regulation office of the department for decades, was a man close to retirement. As one could imagine, the manager, whose name was Claude Tremblay, was happily idle with his new duties, now supervising two additional clerks, added to the two who were already processing applications for leather goods other than footwear. Tremblay was renowned in the office for his bizarre behaviour, his afternoon naps, his daily bouts of inebriation, which usually started across the street at Blair's Bar and lasted under he fell asleep behind his desk until it was time to go home. In addition, there were his occasional shouts of unintelligible complaints, usually about his treatment by senior management.

In that regard, Tremblay, who had worked for the import regulation office since the early 1950s, was resentful of a career that had stood still while others who he thought less deserving than him had been promoted. To Tremblay, it happened too often and, with the arrival of two more clerks under his command, may be happening again. The two agency clerks transferred to his section, regardless of their temporary status, appeared to Tremblay to be a threat, mainly because they all seemed to have some sort of derisive quality. Plainly put, Tremblay did not like them, particularly when compared to the two permanent clerks who were already working for him. He imagined that the new clerks would undermine him somehow, for example by either ignoring his directions or not overlooking his obvious character flaws. On the other hand, the clerks who had been working for Tremblay had ignored his shortcomings for years. In fact, most if not all of the permits that were eventually issued in his name were authorized not by Tremblay himself but by the two faithful clerks who reported to him.

On their first day in the footwear section, the two clerks were quietly introduced to their new boss who never even stood up to shake their hands. It quickly become obvious that the two new clerks were to follow the same procedure with their new boss as their current two subordinates had. The younger of the two veteran minions, a guy who looked to be in his late twenties and whose name was Guy, told the two of them pretty well what everyone in the entire office already knew. "Try to agree with whatever he says, no matter how ridiculous. Particularly in the afternoon, when he comes up with some really crazy stuff ---- you know, after he's been drinking and before he's had his nap." Guy's colleague, an older man named Maurice, was standing beside him, nodding in agreement the entire time. Guy then went on to explain the job, again reminding the new recruits of the conditions of import permit issuance, and handed each of them a stack of applications, telling them to access their veracity and recommend which of the applications should be issued as permits. The two new clerks smiled to each other, agreeing that the job was relatively undemanding, a conclusion that they shared with Guy and Maurice. Guy, however, contradicted their positive impression of their new duties by mentioning its most unpleasant aspect, handling the complaints of aggrieved importers. Under no circumstances, Guy warned them, were they to refer any enraged importer to higher authority, including most particularly Claude Tremblay, who reacted to any importer's complaint by either slamming the telephone down or ripping up any letters of protest. They were, however, to assure importers that their disagreements would be taken into account by senior management. Guy and Maurice said that they would get used to using constant excuses to respond to complaints. Mike called them outright lies. All four of the clerks in the footwear section laughed.

Like a lot of his colleagues, a more consequential circumstance for Mike was the language problem not only within the footwear section but also the import permit office in general. The Canadian Government was bilingual, meaning that the working languages of its departments were supposed to be English and French. There were of course a lot of exceptions. Like a lot of Anglophones working for the government, the two new clerks were not even close to being bilingual while Mr. Tremblay and his two subordinates, Guy and Maurice, were so blessed. That meant that they spoke to each other in French but to the two new clerks, not to mention most of the rest of the office, in English. Even worse, Mike himself was the least bilingual, lucky to say hello in French and almost proud of the fact. That must have added to Tremblay's indignation, if not his anger. On the other hand, Tremblay seldom had to interact with the new clerks, that task left to his two long serving subordinates. In any event, the situation added to the tension of the situation although over time, things seemed to relax a bit. As difficult as it was for him, Tremblay seemed to gradually accept Mike and his coworker, mainly because the addition of the two new clerks, despite the increase in the section's workload, did not require him to limit his luncheon drinking or forego his afternoon siestas. In other words, nothing had changed for Tremblay.

For the first two weeks of his stint in the footwear section, Mike went to work everyday worried that he would get a visit from Mrs. Crabb, who was head of human resources for the office. He thought, in fact he was almost convinced that he might be laid off entirely or transferred to another section of the office, at first his paranoia so significant that he seriously considered looking for another position. Over time, maybe a month, his anxiety diminished and he grew to accept the situation, noting that as long as he stayed away from Mr. Tremblay, not speaking to him in particular, he had no concerns with the circumstances at work. In fact, he began to enjoy his duties, even volunteering for frequent overtime hours, spending additional hours, without pay by the way, joined by not only his coworker in the footwear section, but by a number of likeminded individuals, college educated clerks who seemed obviously overqualified. Management was more than pleased although their fellow clerical staff, the co-workers who were there before the office was expanded to its current size, were initially disgruntled, often complaining to each other, particularly about the overtime. On the other hand, the recently hired clerks were providing enough additional work to allow the veterans to take it easy, or so some of them thought. Further, when they discovered that the recent hires were not receiving overtime pay, they were both appeased in a curious way and mystified. No time and half? No one could quite figure that out.

~~~~~~~~~~~~~~~~~~~~~~~~~~~~~~~~

Aside from the work itself, there was a fair amount of socializing among the group of clerks putting in unpaid overtime five evenings a week, not to mention the occasional Saturday. It was predictable therefore that romantic entanglements would develop, sometimes temporarily, sometimes even longer term. Although Mike was attracted to at least one of his clerical colleagues, a former kindergarten school assistant named Linda, he never got the opportunity to begin any sort of liaison with her, an affair that she was rumoured to be conducting with a married lawyer who also worked elsewhere in the office a serious obstacle. Still, the overtime clerks, including Linda would go out for dinner and drinks most evenings after their additional shifts, most of which lasted three or four hours. They usually went to the basement cafe in the Holiday Inn, next door to the C.D. Howe Building. They would have dinner, they would enjoy drinks, they would discuss the insanity of the previous day's activities and make fun of their bosses, some of them anyway.

Aside from ridiculing their supervisors, some of whom would no doubt reciprocate with their own complaints about them, they would discuss their plans for the future, that is if they had any. Specifically, whether the office in general offered them any career possibilities. In this regard, each one of them had filed applications for employment with the government, including they assumed Industry, Trade & Commerce (ITC). Fact was that a majority of them had university degrees, which were now pretty well useless in the current jobs but did qualify them for other jobs. There were, however, a number of officers, presumably with university degrees, who had higher level jobs. A couple of them actually supervised some of the clerks who were now pondering whether they could consider actually pursue one of those higher level jobs.

It was obvious that Mike and most, if not all of his colleagues, were optimistic about higher positions, even the possibility of careers, which so far had eluded them, realities which explained their current occupations as short term officer clerks. In Mike's case, his departure from the Bank of Montreal several years ago the last opportunity he had to launch one, he realized that unless he started a career shortly, he could find himself either looking for short term positions for the foreseeable future, whether white collar, blue collar or no collar at all. Aside from seemingly working harder than their more experienced colleagues and working unpaid overtime, Mike and his friends thought that they were impressing senior management by their general behavior around the office, not to mention the fact that they all dressed better. Like many of the other temporary clerks, Mike started showing up for work attired in a shirt and tie. That probably influenced senior managers although it annoyed the hell of the old timers.

***

It was an office Christmas party, two weeks before the day. Maybe a hundred people working in the import permit bureau, not to mention individuals from other offices in ITC, were invited to the gathering. It was held in the function room on the top floor of a downtown apartment building. Officers above a certain level was asked to contribute $50 to $100 each while all others had to pay $20 to gain admittance. Escorts were allowed but not encouraged. Predictably, this entitled every misogynist in the office to behave badly, that was before the term had any meaning. So, like similar festivities held by government departments and companies for the past decades, excessive drinking and sexual harassment, as obvious or as subtle as it may have seemed, was not only permitted but almost required. By the time Mike arrived, a good number of the celebrants, mainly if not exclusively men having started drinking at lunch, were already inebriated, weaving through the crowd, pretending to dance to the disco music playing in the room, pawing clerks and secretaries, and attempting to entertain their fellow party goers with off colour pranks and witticisms. One of the drunken merrymakers was sleeping undetected under one of the tables.

In addition to such amusements, a couple of women from the office had made up a game based on a Sadie

Hawkins dance. Each woman was to pick a man's name out of a bowl and then ask him to dance. According to the hostess who introduced the game, the dance would prompt the festivities to begin in earnest. Hoping for Linda to pick his name out of the bowl, an unlikely scenario in view of the fact that there were maybe fourty to fifty men's names in that bowl, Mike watched as women began to pick men's names, each written on a piece of paper about the size of a business card. Once every man was selected, whose names were included in the bowl, the women began to approach the men on the cards and the music started. A woman named Brenda, a secretary in the legal sector, walked up to him and asked him if he wanted to dance with her. He agreed. Mike was surprised that the woman, who was well into middle age, had attended the party. Mike wondered what Brenda was doing at the party, at her age. While they danced, they didn't speak except to introduce themselves to each other. They knew who the other was but had never spoken or been formally or informally introduced. During their almost silent dance, Mike was looking at Linda who apparently had drawn a guy named Barry who worked in the agricultural section. He had seen her dance several times during the evening although with different partners. But he lost sight of her after a while. As for Mike, he may have danced with every second lady at the party, including head of human resources Mrs. Crabb, another surprising attendee. Unlike some others, he did not end up finishing the evening.

Others did, however, the rumours being that there were a number of would be philanderers who were able to persuade various female colleagues, whose foolishness, aided by too much liquor perhaps, placed them in situations which they would not have otherwise been. There was gossip that several couples were seen leaving certain downtown hotels the next morning. Evidently, to most guys the big winner in the Sadie Hawkins sweepstakes was a guy named Bill, who, in addition to being a well known womanizer around the office was a director in the bureau, was asked to dance by a woman named Donna. Aside from being a secretary, Donna apparently performed as a stripper in a club called Rick's Place on Bank Street. That explained why she was often late for work ----- her shift ended at one o'clock in the morning. Her fellow secretaries often complained about having to take over her work when she was tardy, which was frequently. In any event, Bill the director was envied, if not acclaimed until the Christmas holidays were over. No one asked about Donna. To many people, she had a salacious reputation anyway, whether deserved or not.

Aside from any prurient stuff, that standard of gossip fairly common in Donna's case, there were a number of other memorable incidents that occurred that evening. Around ten o'clock in the evening, a clerk named Howard dumped an entire tray of party sandwiches on a man named Wilson Forsyth, who was in charge of the file room. He claimed that his official title was Chief, an absurdly pompous designation for a man who supervised two file clerks, his official title being manager. Everyday, he wore the same blue three piece suit, an overly formal outfit for a man who oversaw the work of two guys who dressed like they were working in a factory, and affected the disposition of an old fashioned school principal. So it was no surprise then that he was pretty well disliked by anyone who came in contact with him. Most of his colleagues wondered about the origin of his employment, the main theory being that his father, or some other relative had recommended him and was still vouching for him. So when his colleagues heard about the clerk named Howard who had befouled Wilson Forsyth's three piece suit with a tray of egg salad sandwiches, he was celebrated throughout the office, at least for a week or so. It was regarded as some sort of political triumph.

One of the other unforgettable episodes involved two obvious rivals within the office, Claude Tremblay and another office manager, a comparatively younger man named Peter Miller. There was Tremblay's dislike for Miller, who was after all younger, much better educated and by god an Anglophone. On the other hand, Miller thought Tremblay was an incompetent drunk who should have been let go years ago. Tremblay, who was inebriated as usual, seemingly barely able to stand up, had accosted Miller early in the evening, without a warning or a reason, he took a swing at him, missed and fell down. Miller stood over Tremblay and attempted to help him up. Miller had gripped Tremblay's right wrist, prompting him to let out a quick yelp. Miller thought almost immediately that Tremblay's right wrist was broken. A number of guests had crowded around Tremblay who now was almost standing. Somebody went to telephone an ambulance while somebody else volunteered to drive Tremblay to the Civic Hospital on Carling Avenue.

Tremblay was being held up by Miller and another gentleman. He now leaned toward Miller and swung his good arm at him. Again, he missed him and hit the floor for the second time. Amazingly enough, a phenomenon then occurred that provided the entire office with chatter for months. Tremblay had managed to break his other wrist, the left one this time. Aside from the circle of men around the groaning Tremblay, it appeared that a majority of the celebrants were unaware of Mr. Tremblay's sudden injuries. Fortunately, two ambulance attendants arrived and were on their way out of the party within fifteen minutes.

It took a few months before Mr. Tremblay, who was replaced by a man named Legault, officially retired after almost fourty years of working for the Government of Canada, including five years spent in the military. He was sporting casts on both wrists for a month.

THEY WERE CALLED COMPETITIONS

It was explained to Mike about five years ago by a chemist named Janice for whom he worked part time in the National Research Council building on Sussex Drive. The two of them became close friends over the four months he had performed janitorial services for her. She told him one afternoon that she was worried because her husband, who also worked for the government, was participating in a competition in which he was a candidate for a better job. After a written examination, during which certain applicants are selected, personal interviews are then conducted by three officials, two representing the office with the job and a third from human resources. Based on this process, which was called a competition, a successful applicant is then determined and the job offered.

According to the government, it was an objective way of awarding government positions, better than the previous practice of providing jobs based on little more than an application and a personal interview. Further, it prevented the kind of nepotism that frequently occurred when government jobs were awarded. Janice said that

Randall, her husband, was particularly anxious about the interview part of the "competition", so much so that he practiced for days, only to abandon the interview after a frightening case of the nerves. For the next job for which he applied, a decision he reached reluctantly and only after the encouragement of Janice, he knew that he would likely have to face an interview. As a result, he was able to persuade the family doctor to prescribe him an anti-depressant. It was either that he explained to Janice or he would have to appear before the "competition" board fortified by alcohol, having been told that vodka was the most effective and least likely to be discovered remedy. Mike left his part time job at the National Research Council before he was able to find out if Randall participated in that "competition" and whether he had been successful.

Two years later, after Mike had joined the Royal Canadian Mint, he was involved in a "competition". He had applied a position as a clerk, filled in the appropriate form, submitted a curriculum vita, a document with which he was unfamiliar and which his wife Sharon had completed for him, and was invited to an interview with Deputy Director White, accountant Plante and some individual who he didn't know. In any event, he answered several ridiculously easy questions, at least as far as he was concerned, and was awarded one of several clerical jobs. The process wasn't called a "competition" at the time, a term that was only applied by the government several years later. The first "competition" in which he did participate was in the very bureau in which he was working, the import permit bureau. There were several permanent clerical positions that were made available by the continuing increase in products that were subject to import permit requirements. Surprisingly, several of the short term clerks, including Mike, who were competing for one of the permanent clerk jobs, were asked to provide to a soon to be retiring manager named Gerard Laflamme, who was appointed responsible for the administration of the "competition", questions that applicants could be asked. It was apparent that Laflamme was not particularly familiar with the duties of the permit clerks, specifically the administration of the regulations on imports of textiles and clothing, footwear, various agricultural products, and in rare instances, endangered species. So he and the other two individuals serving on the board had to be furnished questions that they could ask candidates for the positions.

Mike did not take the assignment very seriously. While he did provide Mr. Laflamme with some proposed questions that could be used, he also included some humorous suggestions just for the hell of it. In other words, a practical joke. Before submitting the proposed questions to Laflamme, he had passed them around the office. Most of his colleagues thought they were a bad idea even though they were entertained. Some of the prank questions included: *i) To issue an import permit illegally, what is regarded as a respectable bribe? ii) Are cauliflowers subject to import permit regulations? iii) How long must you talk to complaining importers before you hang up? iv) Do you have to wear a tie to meet with an importer? and v) If an importer buys you lunch, do you have to eat it?* While Laflamme was mildly entertained by Mike's attempts at comedy, he had to keep his reaction to himself, pretending to censure Mike when the other two board members became aware of his foolishness.

Despite his six months of experience with issuing permits, first for imports of clothing and then for footwear, he was not successful in the "competition". Even though he was understandably disappointed, Mike could not quite determine why he was not awarded one of the four clerical jobs that were awarded by Mr. Laflamme and his board. On the other hand, he and several other individuals, including a woman who was supposedly friendly with Mrs. Crabb of human resources, were relatively certain that the bureau would be looking to hire several permanent clerks shortly, not to mention several more policy officers, a higher level of employee. Mike was only discouraged for a couple weeks, after which time he forgot his previous failure, which he began to regard as an audition, and waited for his next opportunity at a permanent position.

He and several of his colleagues, including Joyce, a fellow short term clerk in the footwear section, would discuss the entire "competition" process frequently. One of the approaches to "competitions" that potential job applicants often pursued was to study for them. Although studying was more likely, if not necessary the more senior the position, even clerical jobs elicited some pre-interview education. In fact, a couple of the colleagues involved in the most recent "competition" had taken days off to study up for it. And that was for a clerical position. Mike and Joyce did not study and did not even consider studying, particularly since Mike had been asked to provide Mr. LaFlamme with questions that could be used in the interviews, questions that were not intended to be amusing.

While two of the clerks who were selected had studied, both Joyce and Mike were still convinced that studying for a written test or an interview was hardly worth the effort. Mike had been told by a fellow clerk named Jean Lesarge that he had studied the act governing the permit regulations, various notices that had been sent to importers against the regulations, and even researched the library for historical material on Canadian export and import regulations to prepare for the "competition". The other clerk who had studied and had been awarded a permanent position was an individual named Wendal "Bud" Denman who worked in an another area of ITC. He was not known by anybody in the bureau. Mike was hardly alone in accepting that studying was hardly warranted. Both Joyce and Mike, most of the other candidates who had an opinion were of the view that those who studied were either not qualified for the job in the first place or were attempting to impress management with their enthusiasm for the job. It became clear, at least to most people in the bureau, that "Bud" Denman had studied for the "competition" in order to impress management. Within weeks, if not a month, he had managed to secure a reputation as one of the most ingratiating individuals in the bureau. In other words, a prominent "ass-kisser".

It was not too long before the bureau ran another "competition" for permanent clerical positions. Fortunately, or so Mike thought, Mr. Laflamme was once again asked to convene the board to consider applicants for several more clerical positions. Mike of course applied, being told by practically everyone, including Joyce in particular, that he was guaranteed to be awarded one of the positions. The bureau had decided to expand the number of people who could qualify to apply for one of the jobs. Rather than limit applications to people who worked in the Department, it was decided to broaden qualifying applicants to anyone working in the government, a verdict that the board soon realized would likely extend the duration of the "competition" from a month or so to at least three months. It did not affect, however, anyone's expectations regarding their chances of being appointed to a permanent position. There were only three candidates, including Mike, who actually worked in the bureau. Two of them were looking for promotions, the clerical jobs paying more money. To both Joyce and Mike, it seemed that both secretaries would have to study to prepare for the board although they also concluded that given their years as secretaries in the bureau would have provided them with considerable knowledge of the policies and operations of the office.

After four months, during which a dozen applicants were interviewed by the "competition" board, three new permanent clerks were appointed, the two secretaries and Mike. The interviews were conducted by a board made up by Mr. Laflamme, who had the obvious experience, a Mr. Wilson who was an executive director and who didn't seem to have any specific duties around the permit bureau, and a woman named Alice Monette, who was an assistant to Mrs. Crabb. As Mike recalled and later conveyed to Joyce and the few fellow workers who were curious about the "competition", the interview was conducted almost verbatim from the one that was conducted four months previously. Mike thought it was strange or ironic or some other term that could convey something peculiar, that he would be successful in one competition after being unsuccessful in another, when both competitions were identical. He brought the thought up with Joyce who suggested, without contemplation of any sort, that the list of applicants was different in the two competitions. He finally concluded that maybe he had just needed the practice.

Within weeks, another curious development emerged. Mike was transferred from the section responsible for the footwear section to the section responsible for issuing textile and clothing permits. It was a larger section than the footwear section, six individuals, four officers and two clerks, compared to only two clerks in the footwear section, which had been reduced in size after the office was satisfied that importers had been allotted their quotas, leaving only Guy and Maurice to administer the import permit system, Joyce and Mike having been transferred to the agriculture and the textile and clothing sections respectively.

Anyway, Mike was now working for the chief of the textile and clothing section, a stern, tough talking older woman named Millicent Thomas who insisted that she be addressed as Mrs. Thomas and not as Ms. Aside from Mike, the other clerk in the section was a guy named Rick Kane, a veteran CR, the designation that the government gave to employees doing clerical. (The others were CO, AT, AS, and ST). Mr. Kane had quite the reputation, having made indolence his principal personality trait. While he had his critics, particularly among management and those colleagues who actually worked hard, he also had his admirers. He played the guitar in the office or listened to a Walkman but seldom did any work, the letters and permit applications piled up on his desk like waste paper. Like anybody who was tight with the union, Kane perpetually thumbed his nose at management, a smirk his usual expression when approached by anyone who wasn't interested in his music, which was limited to an incomprehensible combination of hard rock and folk music, his complainants about his treatment at work, or his favorite topic, the union. Regarding the latter, it was obvious to almost everyone in the office that he seldom did any work, his reputation known well beyond not only the bureau. In fact, he had admirers among the department's clerks, many of whom were particularly impressed by his ability to take advantage of every regulation in the book to avoid work. The rumour was that Kane had filed more grievances with the union than seemed possible.

It soon became clear to Mike that his new position working for Mrs. Thomas was to be a little different than his previous position in the footwear section. It reminded Mike of his short term stint as an efficiency expert in Heath and Welfare. Mrs. Thomas instructed Mike to provide Rick Kane with minor statistical tasks, which he had to complete within specific deadlines, all to be conveyed in writing. In addition, Mike was to observe and report on Kane's activities within the office. He was going to work on a stakeout, just like police and private detectives on television. Initially, he felt like a creep. Even though the target of his surveillance was hardly reputable, he still felt a little guilty about the task. On the other hand, despite jobs Mike had in which he was witness to co-workers exploiting their jobs not to work, he was reminded of his part time Christmas job at the post office or who most of the time avoided work as if it was infectious.

On his first day in his new position, he and Kane were called into Mrs. Thomas's office so that she could inform her two subordinates of her intentions. Predictably enough, Kane immediately objected to the scheme and demanded to know why he was being singled out for such treatment. He quickly altered the expression on his face, from his customary smirk to something edging on shock, if not rage. He then leaned forward toward Mrs. Thomas.

"What are you talking about, Millie, why tell this rookie here to watch me, why tell anybody to watch me?", the tone in his voice growing intense, like he was prepared to do something physical. Mike immediately recognized that Mrs. Thomas didn't like to be addressed by her Christian name, particularly by a subordinate like Rick Kane.

Mrs. Thomas responded to Kane's challenging inquiries. "You now why, Mr. Kane. You know how many grievances you've filed against me and you know why you filed them. I have always expected and still expect you to work." She reached across her desk, slapped her fists on its surface and continued after a short interval. "I'll bet that you're the laziest clerk in the department. How many times have I given you an assignment, like checking quotas, answering an importers' letters or returning telephone calls, and you just never did them. Instead I find you playing your guitar or listening to music on your damn cassette player. When you weren't working, you were phoning in sick or claiming some vacation days that you you didn't have. That's why I've asked Mr. Butler here to surveil you and your work. I'm tired of worrying about you, tired of answering human resources about your grievances."

Kane just laughed in a dismissive sort of way, "If you don't like me filing grievances, then leave me alone. Come on, Millie, you just don't like me, you never have, maybe it's because of the union, maybe you just don't like unions." Mike was not surprised. He thought that Mrs. Thomas probably wasn't either. Kane continued, "You know that there are plenty of people working in this place, maybe even working for you, that are just as lethargic as I am." Mrs. Thomas was surprised to hear Kane use the word "lethargic".

Mrs. Thomas leaned back from her desk, spread her hands, and concluded their discussion, such as it was. "Well, no matter how you feel, Mr. Kane, I'm asking Mr. Butler here to keep an eye on you for a while, at least until I'm sure about you or you're sure about me." As they left her office, Kane gave him a look that was somewhere between a threat and a joke. Mike didn't know whether Mrs. Thomas noticed.

The surveillance project regarding Rick Kane began properly, almost bureaucratically. Sure, Mike would have to negotiate regarding the deadlines that were established for the various tasks that Mrs. Thomas was to give Kane. In addition, Kane invariably asked for additional explanations for even the most simple of tasks, hoping, he thought, that Mrs. Thomas would grow tired of the entire enterprise. She didn't. As for the deadline complaints, she expected that and had told Mike to give Kane a 20 percent allowance. With that, Kane was not able to meet the deadlines, almost all deadlines given extensions, over the first few weeks. He complained of course, even though all the tasks could easily have been completed in half the time that Mrs. Thomas had originally given him. Still, despite all their efforts but due to all the procrastinating and nonsense, Mrs. Thomas was to abandon her plan to straighten out Rick Kane in little more than a month. Mike figured that Kane had managed to somehow use his position in the union to persuade Mrs. Thomas to drop her vendetta against him, which was what the latter used to call it. Mike was relieved.

<hr />

Before plans for the next office Christmas party were considered, Mike graduated to seriously pursuing the Commerce Officer category after participating in two "competitions" regarding several positions in that classification. It was apparent that the office was expanding the professional caliber of its employees, believing that most of the clerks who had joined the place over the past year or so should be promoted before they were lost to other government departments. Most of them were obviously competent, more competent they concluded than most of the veterans that had been working in the office for many years. Mr. Andrews, the Director General of the entire office, had been encouraging the managers who worked for him to arrange "competitions" in order to hire more Commerce Officers, a project that he assigned to two senior managers, Bill Turner and Victor McNamara, both of whom had experience with running "competitions". When they got over one hundred applicants, even though again candidates were limited to ITC employees, they decided to run two separate contests, before two distinct boards, with two different groups of applicants. On the other hand, both groups would be asked the same questions, at least the same written questions, although the personal consultations would be understandably different, simply because each of the two "competition" boards were to be comprised of three different people.

After passing the written examination, Mike was chosen to sit before the board to be led by Bill Turner who was joined by Lawrence Parks, who was a senior Commerce Officer in the U.S. Trade Development Office, and a personnel associate from the human resources department for the same division, a woman named Elaine Nugent. Mike was generally acquainted with all three members of that board although that wasn't much of an advantage. Again, as he had declined before either of the boards before which he had appeared, he did not do any studying prior to the "competition" boards itself. Although he was not successful in the "competition", he was educated in the approach he should take in any future "competitions, particularly ones which were assessing candidates for better positions. Although he did not come across any situations which might fit his newfound theory, he realized one approach which might prove a drawback in any future job interview. He had taken note of the reaction the board had when Mike attempted to answer a question to which he had no answer by attempting an easily detected falsehood. It is the kind of question that only someone with an education in economics could even have attempted to answer. Mike fumbled through a response that he thought was absurd even after he provided it. So did the board, apparently. One of them actually rolled her eyes with a theatrical flourish. The advice was useful. He would remember not to fabricate phony answers to any questions posed by board members in any future "competitions".

It was several months later when Mike got another opportunity to emerge from the clerical to the CO category. In view of his previous experience with "competitions", particularly his most recent one, he was confident that he would be successful. In addition, the human resource officer, Elaine Nugent, was also a member of the most recent board. He therefore fully expected to breeze through the "competition" process without any difficulty. Still, the ease with which he answered most of the board's questions was surprising, even volunteering to expand on his responses, an unnecessary elaboration that annoyed at least one of the board members who often tried to interrupt Mike when he begin to embroider his comments. Despite one board member's reservations about his audacity with his answers, Mike easily won the competition, which had been limited to filling only that one position.

The intention for which the "competition" was

conducted was to fill a position in the overall policy division of the import permit bureau. It was a new position for which a general knowledge of import permit regulations was required, a prerequisite for which Mike was conspicuously qualified, having worked for both the footwear and clothing sections. The division itself was generally well respected, the intellectual heart of the bureau, which was constituted to advise the bureau on policy matters relevant to its operation. It was an enviable place in which to work, not having to deal with the minutiae of administering the government's import policy, the demands of domestic producers, the complaints of exporting countries, and the complaints of importers. Its director was a lawyer named Talbot and the division included a legal assistant, two statisticians, one of whom never used a calculator, a clerk, a secretary and now another general policy officer. Mike would be joining a young woman named Catherine Major who so impressed Mr. Andrews and other senior managers that they often suggested that her future was extremely bright. Within a couple of months, Mike and Catherine had became fairly friendly, so much so that she started to refer to him as "my clerk", an appellation that she often used. Aside from her obvious fondness for him, she also managed to convince Mr. Talbot to allow her to employ Mike as her executive assistant, an exclusive arrangement that did not seem to bother Mike at all despite the occasional ribbing he would receive from colleagues.

COUNTERFEIT PERMITS

He was still working for Catherine when a scandal of sorts emerged in the bureau. As an audit procedure, import permits used to enter regulated goods at the border were returned to the bureau to determine the specific quantities covered by the import permits issued by the bureau. They would then be compared to the permits issued and appropriate quota adjustments would be made. The impropriety, if that's what it was, was that copies of certain permits started to arrive in the office, a clerk named Ester accepting them, that were not issued by the office. The implication was clear, that there were import permits being used to clear regulated goods, in this case cheese, at the border that were not issued by the ITC import permit people. It was obvious that someone, possibly in the section of the bureau that issued import permits governing agricultural products, had liberated blank permits that were then somehow properly completed and used to enter goods at the border.

As an initial step, discovery of the fake permits precipitated office management to order Mr. Talbot's policy division to investigate the bogus import permits in order to determine the responsible individual and to determine whether there were other fakes that could be used to clear certain imports at the border. Under the supervision of Catherine Major, Mike and Ester were assigned to investigate recent import permits to clear regulated goods returned to the office by Revenue Canada after being used at the border. The purpose would be to determine the extent of the problem, that is whether other counterfeit import permits had been used. Senior management, including Director General Andrews in particular, was concerned that the RCMP would have to be brought in to investigate unless the office itself could somehow provide an answer. Andrews and other members of senior management, including Mr. Talbot in particular, were concerned that the import permit problem would reflect badly on the performance of their jobs. There was a serious pressure coming from senior management.

Mike and Ester went to work going through boxes of used import permits, all of which were dated to the beginning of the current year. Ester had recently taken over the auditing of the import permits returned to the office by Revenue Canada from retired military officers who were initially hired to visit customs brokers who had issued the permits on behalf of ITC in the first place. While she was normally a generally petulant employee, Ester seemed suddenly enthused when Talbot told her that she was now supervising Mike in the audit of the import permits, looking for permits that were not officially issued by ITC. Ester had not noted any specific errors in the details between the fraudulent permits and any legitimate import permit. According to her, and pretty well anyone else familiar with the detailed specifications of an import permit, it could be difficult to determine that any permit provided to any Revenue Canada officer at the border was in fact bogus.

The only clues, if you could call any example clues, were the import permits that were not issued by the department.

Over the first three weeks of investigating the permits returned by Revenue Canada, Ester and Mike found four counterfeit permits, three covered shipments of cheese and one covering milk powder. Three of them were entered by a Montreal company that was not normally in the business of distributing cheese. The other importer declared on the phony entry documents was also a Montreal company which apparently did not exist at the time of the importation. While somewhat confounded by the facts, if not slightly embarrassed, Revenue Canada officials claimed that they were not surprised that mistakes were made, noting that thousands of shipments entered the port of Montreal every day. The senior management of the import permit office did not accept the explanation and ordered Ester and Mike to continue their investigation.

As for the investigation itself, Mike conducted his clerical efforts with some alacrity, his interest in the project based on his enthusiasm for detective stories, which he related to the permit investigation. In addition, his mentor, Catherine Major, had not been unhappy with Mike's new assignment, hoping that any success in which Mike would ultimately participate would reflect well on her. After all, she had originally recommended him for the job, being "her clerk" after all. On the other hand, aside from being encouraged with her responsibility for supervising Mike, Catherine was not as motivated as either Ester or Mike were, seeing the project as just another one of her duties, most of which she considered tedious. This special project, such as it was, required Ester to pay special attention to the permits she was usually auditing. Fact was that errors for which the two of them were now searching were one of the details she looked for. Most of the factors which Ester was responsible for auditing involved the names of the importer, the exporter, the product, its quantity and value of the importations, all the details that defined her job as a clerk.

As for Mike, he was only responsible for checking that import permits used to clear the goods at the border matched import permits that had been legitimately issued by the Department. In the first three weeks of their investigation, they found four bogus import permits used to improperly clear goods at the border. After their initial discoveries, it took the two clerks another month to find another fraudulent import permit. This one covered a comparatively large shipment of cheese which had entered through the port of Montreal. As with the other four bogus permits, most of the details of the permit were phony except for the classification of the product, the quantity as well as the value of the shipment. They could find no valid import permit issued by the office that matched the documents submitted with Revenue Canada.

Unfortunately, after nearly two months of review, ITC lawyers and RCMP investigators, who were eventually asked to join the search, did not find any clues that could identify the individual or individuals who originated and administered the scheme to import regulated products, particularly dairy products, using fraudulent import permits. After several weeks of investigation, the RCMP decided to tap the telephones of some of the employees of the office, particularly those individuals who worked in the section that issued import permits for agricultural products. The section was comprised of a chief named Patricia, two officers including Mike's friend and former associate from the footwear section Joyce, three clerks and a secretary, all of whom had their telephone extensions wiretapped. Everyone in the section but a clerk named Barry were disturbed by the RCMP intrusion into their telephone conversations. As for Barry, he was mildly fascinated by the process being pursued by the police who, on the other hand, were generally bored by their investigation. In addition, several of the officers were annoyed not only by having to listen to tapes of telephone conversations between the staff in the agricultural section and presumed importers, customs brokers, business associations and maybe another government departments, most particularly agriculture, but also by Barry's constant questioning of their progress in their investigation, which was minimal.

Gossip around the office was rife. The most conspicuous theory, which was accepted by most of the people in the office, was that the offense was committed by someone who either worked there or had a relationship with someone who worked there. Regarding the latter, Mike was one of the few office workers who believed that somebody who had something to do with supplying blank import permits to the office was somehow responsible for the fraudulence. On the other hand, the few who actually accepted that conjecture also had to deal with the likelihood that all of the employees who worked at the office's printing company were unknown. In addition, the identity of the printing company itself was also unknown and its security measures that were applicable to the printing of import permits were virtually impenetrable, or so thought anyone who had pondered the thesis that the printing company was somehow to blame. In any event, neither theory seemed to make any progress with the RCMP. As one Sergeant Ryan reported to Director General Andrews, the police had not made any progress in solving the case of the bogus import permits. Mike suspected that the RCMP were not likely terribly interested in getting to the bottom of the import permit controversy anyway.

***

Within several months, the office moved from the CD Howe building downtown to the Lester B Pearson building on Sussex Drive, the reason being that the permit office along with a number of offices was being transferred from ITC to Foreign Affairs, it being the last ITC office to be relocated. With respect to the counterfeit import permits, the RCMP had discontinued its investigation, having concluded that someone had somehow managed to misappropriate blank permits from the office's supply, sell them to importers who would then fill them and then use them to import products covered by the act. However, they were unable to identify anyone against whom any sort of charge, criminal or otherwise, could be laid. In other words, they could not prove anything. They therefore abandoned the pursuit of the fraudulent import permit scheme.

SOMEONE DISAPPEARING

His name was Steve Graham, a balding, bespectacled man who had worked for ITC since the he left high school in 1956. He worked for Mrs. Millicent Thomas as an import permit officer in the textile and clothing section. Mike was familiar with him for several months before he reported to Mrs. Thomas after he won a "competition" for a commerce office. He was known around the office as a solitary individual. He didn't socialize with anyone except for his indolent colleague Rick Kane, didn't speak much to anybody but Kane, Mrs. Thomas, and whoever with whom he was compelled to socialize. In other words, people seeking information from him on the telephone or otherwise. Accordingly, most, if not all of his colleagues in the office regarded Steve Graham as a strange, a melancholy middle age guy. Most of his colleagues generally stayed away from him.

So when he was absent from the office for almost a week, no one seemed to be aware of the fact, his only known friend Rick Kane hadn't been in the office for at least two weeks, which was not unusual. Mrs. Thomas was only mildly concerned, the absence of Graham and Kane from the office hardly a complication to the operation of her section since the two of them didn't do any work anyway. She had the section's secretary, a younger woman named April, temporarily take over Graham's work without losing any productivity. Mrs. Thomas thought that maybe she could finally discard the two of them, an ambition that she had pursued for several years. After the fifth day of Steve Graham's absence, Mrs. Carole Graham telephoned the office, asking for her husband. She eventually spoke to Mrs. Thomas.

According to Mrs. Graham, she and her husband Steve had been separated for several months. He had moved out but they stayed in touch, he checking in religiously every couple of days. She told Mrs. Thomas that she hadn't heard from her husband in a week and wanted to know if he was at work. Mrs. Thomas told her that Graham hadn't appeared in the office for a week and she couldn't get in touch with him. He wasn't answering his home telephone and she didn't know where he lived. Mrs. Thomas then asked Mrs. Graham if her husband could be reached at any other telephone number. Mrs. Graham replied that she didn't know of one. She did suggest that he sometimes hung around at a local tavern. She said that maybe Mrs. Thomas might consider checking with the tavern if she was looking for him. She declined.

Before passing any of this information to senior management, Mrs. Thomas asked Mike, not Ester who would likely have complained about the task, to search his desk to determine whether there were any hints as to his current location. The thought of possibly searching Steve Graham's current residence occurred to management although no one seemed to know where he now lived. Even his wife didn't know where he was living. She suggested that maybe his friend Rick from work might know. Even

if they could contact Kane--- he wasn't in the office ----
Mrs. Thomas thought that it was unlikely that Rick Kane
would tell them where Graham now lived, even if he knew.
He would have thought that it was some sort of union trick.
Mrs. Thomas concluded that she had no choice but to ask
Mike to search his desk.

Mike spent an hour or so going through Steve Graham's
desk. He thought the assignment, which some of his
colleagues thought inappropriate, would be interesting, as
if he would find something that would assist the office in
finding him. Surprisingly, there was little in the five drawers
of the desk, which was an older wooden model with a lot of
marks on its surface. There was a desk organizer, an empty
paper tray, a cup in which three pens sat, and a telephone on
the desk. In the bottom drawer on the left side, there were
a number of file folders in which Graham was keeping a
number of letters and receipts regarding various transactions,
including a new suitcase. Above that drawer was a smaller
drawer in which pens, pencils, a tape dispenser, a stapler,
paper clips, an eraser and a bottle of liquid paper were kept.
In the lower drawer on the right side of the desk were four
liquor bottles, two half full and the other two empty, all
vodka, while in the upper right drawer was a bunch of
cigarette papers, scattered weed flakes and a pile of pills
that could be either aspirin, cold tablets or various medical
prescriptions. There was powder that could have been some
illegal substance.

The contents of the thin middle drawer did reveal
several clues as to Steve Graham's location. There was a small
telephone index book which Mike noted that several of the

entries included unfamiliar area codes, a couple of unused import permits that looked like they were originally issued at least a year ago, several faded transparencies of American Express travelers cheques and some change. He reported to Mrs. Thomas who thanked him and said that she would pass the information to Director General Andrews who would then presumably provide it to the ITC legal council, a man named Benjamin, who had taken over responsibility for the case when the RCMP dropped it. The RCMP had concluded that there was no evidence of any crime by Graham, including the fraudulent import permits, of which almost two dozen had been used to clear goods at the border over the past few months. The importers, and there were several, who used the bogus permits to enter goods at the border, had been charged with violations of the import permit legislation, calling the permits "unfortunate errors" or blaming their customs brokers. As for the source of the phony permits, depending on which importer or broker was being interrogated, the government employees who claimed to be working in ITC, Foreign Affairs, Agriculture Canada or Revenue Canada were identified although all their names were later found out to be fictitious. In addition, the telephone numbers that the importers and brokers claimed had been used by the supposed government contacts were public telephones. Although none of these so-called clues led to any firm conclusion, most of his office colleagues, the very few friends he may have had and maybe even his wife Carole, had decided that he had sold blank import permits to importers who couldn't acquire them legitimately, decided that he had built enough capital and then disappeared. There was, however, the matter of proof. No one had any.

Several months later, a woman named Valerie, who was working as a clerk in the export permit section, was successful in a "competition" to replace Steve Graham, the office having abandoned any possibility that he would return. For a reason that he could never explain, Mike Butler had been asked to sit on the board.

His name was Randolph Rizzo. He had worked with Steve Graham years ago when the department was called National Revenue. Though he was retired for several years, he heard about the counterfeit import permit scam one Friday afternoon during a gathering of former and current Customs officials at the Chateau Lafayette in the Byward Market. After several quarts of Molson Ex, Mr. Rizzo, who had worked as a Customs official first at the port of Montreal and then at headquarters in Ottawa for almost fifty years, offered a theory about the permit fraud. He suggested that Mr. Graham, who had known Mr. Rizzo for almost thirty years, might have used the fraudulent import permits himself rather than providing them to a e third party. He then vanished, not having been seen by anyone in more than six months. The Customs officials around the table all agreed that it was fascinating hypothesis. They all laughed.

Printed in the United States
by Baker & Taylor Publisher Services